VICTORIAN SUMMER

It's 1897 and while England is celebrating Queen Victoria's Diamond Jubilee, the Baker sisters have decisions to make. Should Ada accept the marriage proposal of Ted Cooke, the miller's son? She has always loved him, yet she can't forget that he met with another girl behind her back. As for Millie, she admires Dr Edwin Carson, but the scheming Julia Pennington, wealthy and beautiful, wants him for herself. Does Millie stand a chance?

CATRIONA McCUAIG

VICTORIAN SUMMER

Complete and Unabridged

LINFORD
Leicester

First published in Great Britain in 2011

First Linford Edition
published 2012

British Library CIP Data

McCuaig, Catriona.
  Victorian summer. - -
  (Linford romance library)
  1. Love stories.
  2. Large type books.
  I. Title II. Series
  813.6–dc23

  ISBN 978–1–4448–1147–6

Published by
F. A. Thorpe (Publishing)
Anstey, Leicestershire

Set by Words & Graphics Ltd.
Anstey, Leicestershire
Printed and bound in Great Britain by
T. J. International Ltd., Padstow, Cornwall

This book is printed on acid-free paper

1

June in Gloucestershire. Could there be any lovelier place in all the world? So Millie Baker wondered as she walked home through the village of Pennington Parva, lingering at every cottage gate to absorb the scent of roses and lavender which filled the air.

The sound of small wheels squeaking broke into her reverie. She swung around to see a young woman approaching, pushing a wicker perambulator along the uneven road.

'Daydreaming, are you?' The girl came to a halt, obviously out of breath.

'Oh, hello, Rose! I didn't notice you behind me.'

'And we all know why that is, I'm sure. It's love, that is!'

Millie pulled a face. 'The only love I'm interested in is love-in-a-mist and love-lies-bleeding, both growing in these lovely gardens. And how is little Ivy Rose getting along?' She bent over the baby carriage, smiling at its little occupant, a pretty child, attired in a starched white frock.

'Well, what about your Ada, then, and Ted Cooke! She's only to say the word and he'd be over to see her in a heartbeat. He's well worth courting, is that one, all set to inherit the flour mill when his dad dies. She could do a lot worse than marry a chap like him.'

'I wouldn't want to see her giving Ted Cooke the time of day. I know he's your cousin, Rose, and I shouldn't speak ill of him to you, but I just can't forgive him for what he did to her.'

'We all make mistakes, Millie.'

'And his was a big one — courting both her and that Jenny Robbins at the same time, if you please. All sorts of promises he made to poor Ada, and she believed every word of it. Then he went walking out with Jenny, and Ada was none the wiser until some gossip in the village spilled the beans to her. That's not the sort of man she wants for a husband, Rose. Why, she'd never be able to trust him. Every time he was making a delivery away from home she'd be worrying in case he was sweet-talking some other poor girl.'

'That's not how it was, Millie, as Ted himself told me. True, he was escorting both of them, but that was before he'd made up his mind it was Ada he wanted. It would have been wrong of him to wed Ada while he had feelings for someone else, and that you can't deny. If only she'd give the poor chap a chance — I know it could all come right in the end.'

'I don't want to fall out with you, Rose,' Millie said firmly, 'but the answer has to be no. He hurt my sister badly.'

Rose shrugged sadly. 'What I don't understand is how the both of them could have taken up with our Ted at the same time, each without the other one knowing.'

'That was easily done, Rose. I live at home and teach at the school all day, but our Ada works up at the Hall, and she only gets a half day off each week, so she doesn't always hear the local gossip — and I'm quite certain that's what Ted counted on.'

Rose looked a little affronted, but sighed. 'Oh, well, she knows where to find him, if she changes her mind. He don't give up easy, that I do know, so she can count on seeing him again. Well, I'd better be off, before my hubby gets in, wanting to know where his tea is.'

Millie stood watching as her old school friend marched off down the village street, bound for home.

Of one thing she was sure; she hoped that Ada would avoid Ted Cooke like the plague. Knowing him, he would probably soon find some other hapless female to latch onto, and then she could forget about him.

Millie sighed. In a way she envied her friend Rose her home life and her darling baby, Ivy Rose. Not that there was anything wrong with her own home, and she also had a career she enjoyed. It was just that she was already twenty-three years old and, in the eyes of the village gossips, she was fast approaching old maid status.

Still — on a day like today, there was no point in wallowing in gloom. The sun was shining and all was well in her world.

⋆　⋆　⋆

When she reached the gamekeeper's cottage where she lived with her parents, she found her mother sitting on the doorstep in the sunshine, shelling peas into an enamel bowl.

'Oh, there you are, Millie! Have a good day, did you?'

'Yes, Mum, thank you, I did.'

'I daresay the youngsters are up to fever pitch with excitement, getting ready for the celebrations?'

Millie laughed. 'I was trying to explain to them what a Diamond Jubilee is all about. Of course, they know who Queen Victoria is, because we have her picture on the classroom wall, and we sing God Save the Queen every day. What they can't get their heads around is that she's been ruling for sixty years. Little Tommy Merridew's jaw dropped — 'Cor, she must be about a hundred!' he told me.'

'Well, seventy-eight must seem ancient to him. What is he, five or six? I know his grandma and she's only in her forties!'

'That's not all he's confused about. We're learning a medley of nursery rhymes to sing on the big day, and he's got the idea that the Queen is coming and we'll be singing directly to her. He'll be so disappointed when she doesn't turn up.'

'The old girl in Pennington Parva — that's a good one! Of course, those Penningtons would think it's only their due, snooty devils, especially that Lady Augusta, all hoity toity!' Fanny Baker wrinkled her nose at the thought.

Lady Augusta Pennington wasn't much liked in the village. She expected the local women to bob a curtsey when they happened to meet, and as Fanny had said, more than once, it was a bit much. It was all very well for the men to doff their caps when they saw her — that was due to any woman, lady or not — but their wives were not in her pay.

'Mr Basil isn't so bad,' Millie remarked, but Fanny wasn't convinced.

'I've finished these peas,' she said, standing up. 'How about you scraping those potatoes for me? I want to go inside and make some apple dumplings. I've just time before your dad gets home.'

Watching her mother at work in the shady kitchen, Millie scraped away at the potatoes, looking around the room as she did so. The scrubbed table, now littered with apple cores and daubed with flour, had six high-backed wooden chairs pulled up to it. Only three of them would be occupied this evening, for Millie was the only one of the children in the Bakers' family still living at home.

Ada was head house parlourmaid at the Hall, and of course she lived in, and just as well, too. Her day began at five o'clock in the morning, and she didn't get to bed until ten o'clock at night, and not even then if the Penningtons were entertaining. It was a long, weary day, and nobody needed a two-mile trudge twice in twenty-four hours on top of it all.

The girls had two brothers, who were long gone. Peter Baker had joined the army at a young age, and goodness knows where he was now. Marching up and down somewhere, Millie thought, resplendent in a bright red uniform.

Jack Baker was far away in Canada. Unable to find work that appealed to him in England, he had gone to seek his fortune in the Dominions and, when last heard from, had been working on the railway, shovelling coal into the furnace of a steam train, and staying in a boarding house by night.

Their father, Abel Baker, was Basil Pennington's gamekeeper. His wife was proud of that. It was a very responsible job, as she never tired of telling all who would listen. It had its drawbacks, of course — what job didn't? He was out in all winds and weathers, and was sure to be stricken with rheumatism in old age, but their cottage came with the job, and it was a good one, cosy and weatherproof. Fanny was a contented woman.

'By the way, I saw Rose Taylor on the way home,' Millie remarked, putting the potatoes in a pot of water. 'Ivy Rose is a real little duck.'

'She'll be crawling by now, I expect, and getting into everything,' her mother said, smiling. 'I'm longing for the day when you and our Ada give me a grandchild or two.'

'Well, I'm sure you wouldn't want to see them yet awhile, what with me and our Ada not being married.'

'Millicent Baker! What a thing to say! Mind you, I do think it's about time you girls were settled down.'

'Chance would be a fine thing.'

'But Ada did have a chance, dear, and it's not gone yet. Don't you think she might make it up with young Ted? He's got good prospects, you know. She'd never want for anything, marrying into that family.'

Millie glared at her mother. 'I've told you, Mum, after what he did to Ada, she wants nothing more to do with him. How could she trust him not to do the same again after they were wed?'

'Oh, well, I expect she knows best, dear. And I suppose the right man will come along for you both one of these days, just you wait and see. In the meantime, you've got a good enough life, teaching at the school, and there's many would rejoice to have the same.'

Millie nodded in agreement. But neither of them had any inkling how quickly things could change — and not for the better, either.

2

The last notes of the piano had died away after morning assembly, and Miss Powell stood up to give the concluding prayer. Millie shepherded her charges into the infants' room and the day of study began, beginning with the dreaded sums.

'Tables first, children,' she announced. Following her lead they began to chant, 'Two ones are two, two twos are four, two threes are . . .'

Although some day she hoped to become a headmistress like Miss Powell, Millie wasn't looking forward to the day when she had to teach arithmetic to the senior pupils. When it came to the eleven and twelve times tables, she was a bit shaky herself.

Having chalked up a group of simple sums on the blackboard, which the youngsters would copy onto their slates, she stood back, hoping for a few moments' peace while they struggled with the work.

'Please, Miss, that's too hard!' a tow-headed child informed her.

'Come now, Johnny Groves, it's simple enough if you use your head and think. Which sum has got you puzzled?'

'All of them, Miss!'

'Nonsense. Let's look at the first one. Six times three. Where have you heard that before? Not five minutes ago. Three ones are three . . . '

'But that's tables, Miss. This is sums.'

Millie sighed. 'Who can tell me the answer?'

A forest of hands shot up, while Johnny scratched his head. It was going to be a long morning, and the hands of the clock were moving as slowly as treacle in January.

Finally she noted with relief that the session was over. 'Reading next, children,' she announced. 'Monitors, give out the reading books please, and we will turn to page nineteen, where we left off last time.'

There was a loud crash in the adjoining room and all eyes turned to the door. Millie jumped at the sound, but whatever had happened, it was none of her business. Presumably Miss Powell would deal with it.

There was a commotion at the door and a child burst in, wild-eyed.

'Really, Gertie! Haven't you ever been told to knock and wait for an answer? Someone might have been standing behind the door and there could have been a nasty accident.'

'But Miss, it's Miss Powell — she fell over, and I think she's dead!'

All eyes were on the speaker now. Millie made a quick decision. 'Heads down, everybody, and stay where you are until I get back. Gertie, you're in charge. Sit here on my chair, and make sure nobody moves. If anyone gets out of their desk you must let me know, and they'll get the cane.'

Millie flew into the next room, closing the door behind her. Miss

13

Powell was lying on the floor, almost covered by a pile of maps and books.

'Are you all right, Miss Powell?' As soon as she'd said it, Millie realised what a silly question it was, but she was in awe of her headmistress, whom she had known since she herself had been a beginner in the infants' room.

As she spoke she began to move the pile of debris aside, watched by the older children, who were all agog to see their fallen teacher on the floor. Nothing so exciting had happened since the day of the big storm, when the roof had leaked buckets of water all over the place.

The older woman stirred. 'I think I've broken my ankle . . . and my head is throbbing. I don't know what happened . . . I opened the map cupboard and everything came tumbling out. Can you help me up, dear? We mustn't frighten the children.'

Millie gulped. Trying to remember what she'd learned at the military first aid lecture she'd attended the previous

14

year, she pulled herself together. *Reassure the patient. Tell them what you're going to do.* That was it.

'We mustn't move you, Miss Powell, in case there are injuries we can't see. I'll try to make you more comfortable while we send for Dr Atwood. In the meantime, perhaps we should send the children outside to play?'

'Certainly not, child. Who is to supervise them in the playground, with both of us in here? Whatever are you thinking?'

Rebuked, Millie turned to face the children. 'I want a really reliable person to fetch Dr Atwood. Is there somebody here I can trust?'

'Pick me, Miss! Pick me!' Chests were thrust out in an attempt to give their owners a look of responsibility. Millie pointed to the tallest boy there.

'You. Tom Frost, is it? What are you going to say to the doctor?'

The boy didn't hesitate. 'Come quick, mister! There's been an accident up the school.'

'I suppose that will do. Now, I need

15

another person to go to the school house and fetch a blanket and a cushion. Bella Curtis, you'll do.'

'Not the red cushion with 'A present from Bournemouth' on it,' Miss Powell muttered. 'Bring the old one from the kitchen chair and the knitted blanket from the couch.'

'I must just pop back and see if everything is all right next door,' Millie said, although in truth there was no sound of an uproar. She went in to find Gertie striding up and down between the rows of four-seater desks, waving the cane in a threatening manner.

'No need for that, Gertie. I'll take that now, thank you. I shall be away for a while longer, so you can read them a story while I'm gone. The Green Fairy Book will do nicely. It's on the shelf behind my desk.'

'What about Miss Powell? Is she going to be all right?'

'I'm sure she will be, children. We've sent for Dr Atwood, and he'll be along presently.'

Millie hoped this would be the case. At this time of the morning he should be holding his surgery, but there was always the possibility that he'd been called away to attend to a farm accident, or some poor woman in labour, who was in difficulties beyond the scope of the midwife.

Having made sure that Miss Powell was covered with her blanket, with her head resting on a shabby cushion, Millie faced the class of older pupils. 'Miss Powell wishes you to draw a map showing the Cinque Ports,' she told them. 'Work neatly, please, and no scribbling. I shall come round in a few minutes to see how you are getting on.'

A scuffle at the door revealed Tom Frost, followed by a tall young man, carrying a black bag. Millie looked up in annoyance, barely taking time to register that the visitor was very handsome indeed, with black curly hair and eyes of a startling blue.

'Tom Frost! Didn't I tell you to fetch the doctor here? Go back at once and tell him he's wanted urgently.'

'It's quite all right, Miss. I am a doctor.' The vision squatted down beside the headmistress, speaking to her in a low, gentle voice.

'I went to Dr Atwood's like you said, Miss.' Tom was anxious to justify his actions. 'He weren't there, but this 'un were. 'I'm Dr Carson', he says, 'and I'll come with you to help your teacher.' I did do right, didn't I, miss?'

'Of course you did, Tom. Now go and sit down. Miss Powell would like you to draw a nice neat map showing the Cinque Ports, please.'

Puzzled, Millie stood in front of the blackboard, waiting for directions. Who was this Dr Carson and just where had he sprung from — and would prim Miss Powell allow herself to be examined by such a young man, and an unknown one at that?

Snatches of conversation came to her ears, as Miss Powell told her story. ' . . . opened the cupboard . . . things came tumbling out . . . fell back . . . '

18

Dr Carson stood up. 'I don't think anything is broken, just a sprained ankle and a bump on the head from hitting the iron frame of that desk there. She'll have to go to bed with a couple of cold compresses, which you can see to, Miss. A couple of the bigger lads can make a bandy chair so that we can get her over to the school house at once.'

'But the children . . .'

'Best to send them all home, I should think. I bet they won't say no to an extra half-day's holiday, eh?'

Cheers went up as Millie told the children they were free for the rest of the day. 'And go straight home, mind. No loitering on the way or your dads might think you're playing truant, and give you a walloping. You can tell your mothers that Miss Powell has had a fall, but that she's going to be all right. Off you go, now, and no running!'

Two of the older boys linked hands in what was known as a bandy chair, making a seat with their arms to carry the shaken Miss Powell from the classroom to her house, while she clung to their shoulders for fear of falling.

'We won't tackle the stairs,' Dr Carson decided, as they deposited the patient on the comfortable couch. 'I must dash now, for I left a room full of patients back at the surgery. I'll call in later to see how things are, Miss Powell. Meanwhile, I'll leave you in this young lady's capable hands.'

Millie blushed. 'I'm Miss Baker, Doctor. I teach the infants.'

'I guessed as much. Well, don't bother to see me out. Just go and get those cold compresses, will you, and apply them to the affected parts.'

Vastly impressed, the two women watched him go.

★ ★ ★

There was much bowing and scraping when Basil Pennington arrived at the gamekeeper's cottage that evening. Fanny Baker made a great display of removing some non-existent dust from a chair before inviting him to sit down, with her husband waiting anxiously in the background.

'You can stop hovering, Baker,' Pennington snapped. 'There's nothing wrong, at least, not on the estate. It's your daughter I've come to see.'

'Our Ada? But isn't she at work, up at the Hall?'

'Ada? I don't think I know her. One of our maids, is she? Can't expect me to know all our staff. That's my wife's province, not mine.'

'I expect it's our Millie he wants,' Fanny said timidly, seeing her husband's puzzled look. He had just arrived home and had no notion of events at the school.

'Millie? What's she done, then?'

But Fanny was saved from answering as Millie entered the kitchen, hesitating as she saw the chairman of the school governors sitting there.

'There you are, Miss Baker. I hear you dismissed the whole school in mid morning. Is that so?'

'The doctor said it was for the best, sir,' poor Millie stammered. 'I had to look after Miss Powell and the children couldn't have been left alone for the rest of the day. It wasn't safe.'

Her parents exchanged glances. 'I'm sorry if Millie has done wrong, sir,' Abel said, frowning, 'but it sounds like she didn't have a choice, not with Dr Atwood calling the shots. I hope she's not to be dismissed on that account.'

'What are you talking about, man?' Pennington demanded. 'I'm here to discuss what's to be done next.'

'Excuse me, but we have all that in hand, sir,' Millie said. Now she knew she wasn't to be blamed for this morning's events, which were outside her control, she spoke with more confidence.

'You have, have you? Let's hear it, then.'

'Well, sir, we thought — that is, Miss Powell said — that we can take my class in with hers and I'll teach them all. The older monitors will help me to keep order. Miss Powell will set the lessons each day, and mark the copybooks at night. Besides, some of the usual lessons have been set aside while we're practising for the Diamond Jubilee celebration.'

'I see. Well, my idea was to lend you my daughter for the duration.'

'Miss Julia, sir? But she's not a teacher.'

'No, but she's had the finest education money can buy. Don't tell me she's not equipped to teach a crowd of village children.'

Millie had the distinct impression that he'd been about to say 'yokels' but had bitten back the word just in time.

As for the spoiled Miss Julia, she might have learned languages and was familiar with classical music, but how did that compare with Millie's training?

Millie had attended the village school, taught by Miss Powell, who had been there since the year dot, although at one time under the leadership of a stern headmaster, Mr Banks. Later, she had been a pupil teacher at the same school, and she had attended night classes

23

in the town. Her present position had been earned through diligent hard work and dedication.

However, aware that her job depended on this man, she forced a meek expression on to her pretty face, and waited for him to speak.

'Well, Miss? What do you say to that?'

'I'm sure Miss Julia is very capable, sir. It's just that some of the children are inclined to play up a bit at times.'

'Then she shall take charge of the infants. She can always read to them, if nothing else. That will leave you free to take Miss Powell's class.'

'Yes, sir.' Millie's heart sank. She was nervous enough about running the school in Miss Powell's absence and trying to keep the older pupils in order, without having Miss Julia there, throwing her weight around. And would she really be in charge at all, or would Miss Julia assume that, as Millie's social superior, she had the right to behave as she saw fit?

'My daughter will be there tomorrow

morning, then, in plenty time for you to show her the ropes. Is that quite clear, Miss Baker?'

'Yes, sir. Thank you, sir.'

'Then there's no more to be said.' He turned to Millie's father. 'Come outside with me, Baker. I want to speak to you about that problem we've got in the spinney. If we don't do something about it soon, it will lead to trouble.'

The door closed behind the two men, and Millie heard no more.

Her mother gave her a timid smile. 'That's one thing settled, then. At least you won't have to run the whole school by yourself.'

'Mmm,' Millie mumbled.

'Why so gloomy? I thought you'd be glad to have help.'

'Help, yes; Miss Julia, I'm not so sure about.'

'Well, as long as she can prevent them from thumping each other, that's a good thing, isn't it?'

'She'll probably turn up wearing one of those fancy frocks of hers, all frills and furbelows, and then she'll cry blue murder if she gets chalk dust on it, not to mention getting touched with sticky infant fingers!'

'Miss Julia is a lady. You can hardly expect her to dress like a governess, in grey alpaca.'

'Mum! Whose side are you on, anyway?'

'Yours, dear, of course. I just think you need to face facts, that's all.'

Millie nodded. She was not at all appeased.

3

As it happened, she need not have worried, for Julia Pennington failed to put in an appearance. Standing at the school gate, surrounded by chattering children, Millie watched the lane for any sign of an approaching vehicle. It was inconceivable that Miss Julia would walk all the way from the Hall; perhaps their coachman or some other servant would accompany her in the trap, ready to return it after her arrival.

'Miss! Miss!' Millie looked down to see a small girl, tugging at her sleeve. 'It's time for the bell. The big hand is on the twelve and the little one is on the nine. Can I ring it, Miss? Can I?'

'In a few minutes, Becky.'

'But we'll be late for prayers, Miss.'

'That can't be helped. We're waiting for Miss Julia and it would be rude to go in without her.'

But after ten minutes had gone by, Millie was forced to give up, Becky was allowed to ring the bell, and the school day started.

In keeping with her original plan, Millie kept the younger children in the main classroom after prayers, and two extra monitors were appointed to help supervise their work.

The clock had just struck eleven when the door opened, and Basil Pennington strode in without warning, causing the assembled children to struggle to their feet in a hurry. Millie frowned horribly at two boys who were slow to respond, and they lumbered themselves to their feet.

'Good morning, Miss Baker. Good morning, children.'

'Good morning, sir!' the pupils chorused.

'Where is Miss Julia? Is she not here?'

'She never come, sir,' a small girl piped up, saving Millie the trouble of giving an immediate answer.

'Nonsense, girl!' Pennington glanced

around the room, as if he expected his daughter to spring out from behind the blackboard. 'Is this true, Miss Baker? Miss Julia hasn't been here at all?'

'No, sir. I mean, yes, it's true.'

'She'll be here tomorrow, or I'll know the reason why.' And so saying, he stormed out, without even saying goodbye.

'He had too much to drink last night, I 'spect,' the same little girl remarked. 'My Pa gets all cross like that of a morning when he's been down the Hare and Hounds.'

Millie tried to hide a smile, and the whole room erupted in laughter.

When the long day was over at last, and the children had gone on their way home, Millie went to report to Miss Powell at the school house.

As she let herself in she heard muted voices, and she was annoyed to find Julia Pennington seated in the best chair, with Miss Powell hobbling about, making tea.

'Let me do that!' Millie cried,

ignoring the visitor. 'You know the doctor said you must keep your poor leg up off the floor!' She snatched the kettle from Miss Powell's hand and she sank down on a hard wooden chair, ready to leap up again if necessary.

'Miss Julia has kindly come to ask after my health,' the headmistress said faintly. Millie was alarmed to see how pale she looked. Should they send for the doctor, perhaps? If only she could decide what was best.

Fortunately that wasn't necessary, for a moment later there was a knock at the door, and the doctor looked in.

'Why, Dr Carson,' Julia simpered. 'How lovely to see you. I was about to leave a note at the surgery, but here you are in person.'

'Are you unwell, Miss Pennington?' Dr Carson asked.

'Fit as the proverbial fiddle, doctor. I was merely making a social call.'

'Let me help you back onto the couch, Miss Powell. You look as if you're ready to collapse,' Dr Carson observed and Millie was delighted when he turned away from Julia Pennington to look at his patient. 'My goodness! You're white as a sheet. What did I tell you about keeping that foot up?'

'When I arrived a minute ago I found Miss Powell on her feet making tea for Miss Julia,' Millie muttered, hoping that her remark would show Julia in a bad light, and feeling not at all guilty about it. It had been a tiring day, and the girl had let her down badly, without even a word of explanation. And here she was, flirting with the doctor.

'Shouldn't it have been the other way round?' Dr Carson asked.

Julia gave a tinkling little laugh. 'Me? Make tea? I wouldn't know how. We have servants to do that sort of thing at home, of course.'

Millie longed to take Julia Pennington by the scruff of the neck, and shake her until her teeth rattled.

'I'm sure Miss Baker could teach you how,' the doctor retorted.

'Oh yes, I'm sure she could.' Julia curved her lips in a smile, but her eyes were cold as she looked at Millie. 'I expect she knows all about those sorts of domestic tasks. Did you know that her sister is one of our house maids?'

Inwardly seething, Millie looked her straight in the eye. 'Your father paid us a visit this morning, Miss Julia.'

'I wonder what he wanted?'

'He was looking for you. We expected you at the school this morning to help with the children, and were worried when you didn't turn up.'

'Oh, were you? I'm afraid I couldn't spare the time. I had to see my dress-maker, although it is rather a nuisance having to make do with these village seamstresses when I need something new in a hurry. I really must make time to get up to London to visit one of the bigger fashion houses. One should try to look one's best at all times, don't you think?'

'And will you be setting off for London tomorrow, or can we expect to see you here?' Millie was aware that she had gone too far, but the reference to her sister had stung.

'I'm not sure. Let's see what the morning brings, shall we? But enough about that.' Julia turned to the doctor, smiling graciously. 'My parents are giving a little sherry party on Saturday evening. Do say you'll come, Dr Carson. It will be a splendid opportunity for you to meet some of the better families from around these parts.'

'Thank you, Miss Pennington. I shall be delighted. Now, if you'll excuse me, I really must be on my way. I have a patient on the outskirts of the village who must be seen without delay.'

'Ah, then you'll be passing the gates of the Hall. I'm sure you'll be kind enough to give me a lift, won't you? Unfortunately I'm on foot, and it's become much too warm for walking.'

Dr Carson grinned wryly. 'Nothing would give me greater pleasure, Miss Pennington, except that I'm on my trusty bicycle. It would give the gossips something to talk about if you were seen to be perching on my handlebars.'

Julia smiled frostily. 'Quite so. Until Saturday, then.'

'And as for you, Miss Powell, do try to do as I say, or you'll hear from me again very soon.' The doctor grinned again, and went on his way.

Thwarted, Julia turned and took her frustration out on Millie. 'Have a care what you say, Miss Baker. If I choose, I can have you dismissed for insolence. I'll thank you to remember that my father is chairman of the school governors. I need only say the word, and you will find yourself without employment.'

'I'm sure it needn't come to that,' Miss Powell interjected quickly, seeing that Millie was about to explode. 'You did rather leave her in the lurch and Mr Pennington did give us to understand that you would be here this morning to assist with the infant class.'

'And you might have sent someone to let me know what was happening,'

Millie said, unable to keep silent.

Julia raised one delicate eyebrow. 'I'm sure I do not need to explain myself to an assistant. I'm here now, so perhaps you, Miss Powell, will tell me what is expected of me tomorrow. Perhaps I can take some of the children on a nature walk — a few obedient children,' she added.

'I've had time to think while I've been lying here, Miss Julia. My poor head is quite better now and it's just this foot that's keeping me at home,' Miss Powell pointed out. 'I'd be happy to teach some of the older children, perhaps ten at a time. I can stay where I am and they can sit on the rug. It won't do them any harm at all, and I daresay they'll enjoy the novelty.'

'Miss Powell, do you really think you should?' Millie asked.

'I shall be quite all right, Millie. I can tackle history or a grammar lesson quite well without the aid of a blackboard. I'm sure I shall manage.'

'I expect that will be best,' Julia

Pennington said. 'After all, I'm certain you don't want your salary docked, so it is in your own interest to return to teaching as soon as possible.' She gave Miss Powell one of her icy smiles. 'In that case, I'll be going. I've wasted enough time over all this nonsense as it is.' And with that, she flounced out, leaving the two teachers to exchange meaningful looks.

'Well!' Millie gasped. 'Would they really cut your salary, Miss Powell?'

The headmistress shook her head. 'Nothing has been said about it, but I wouldn't put it past Mr Pennington. The governors would be within their rights, I suppose. There can't be any jobs in England where people are paid to stay at home with their feet up.'

'The parents would be on your side, I know. You've taught here for more than thirty years. You even taught some of them as children, when you were a beginner like me.'

Miss Powell smiled sadly. 'I'm sure I'd have their sympathy, but they couldn't do anything about it, other than muttering behind closed doors. There's something you have to remember, Millie dear, and that is that most men hereabouts owe their livelihood to Basil Pennington. It's as Miss Julia says; he holds the power in his chubby little hand. Men with families to feed must watch their p's and q's.'

★ ★ ★

Fanny Baker echoed this sentiment when she heard Millie's story. 'But I expect that Miss Julia simply spoke in the heat of the moment and she's forgotten all about it by now.'

'Well, she did seem a bit cross with poor Dr Carson, when he refused to give her a lift home.'

'As if he could! A fine figure she'd make on the front of his bicycle, showing all her petticoats! Mr Basil would have something to say about that, I imagine.' Millie's mother laughed.

Then, serious all of a sudden she

added, 'Tell me more about this Dr Carson . . . good-looking, is he?'

'I can't say I noticed,' Millie said primly, pushing her chin out firmly.

'Go on with you! A girl your age, not interested in an eligible young man?'

'Oh, Mum!'

'Don't you 'oh, Mum' me, Millicent Baker. A fine catch he'll make for someone. I've heard that he's here to stay. Dr Atwood is getting on a bit, and I've heard that after that turn he had this past winter he thought he'd better slow down a bit. Young Carson has come to help him out in the practice, and if he does well I've no doubt he'll be offered the chance to buy a partnership, with a view to taking over when old Atwood's day is done.'

'How do you know all this, then?'

'I heard it from Polly Dawes, when I went to market. Her second cousin is the old doctor's housekeeper, and she should know how the land lies, if anyone should. So you can set your cap at young Carson, even if you haven't noticed what he looks like!'

'As far as I can see, Miss Julia's already done that,' Millie said sharply. 'And anyway, you've always told me never to run after a chap. The men like to make their own running, you always said.'

'Ah, but since when did you ever do as I told you?' Fanny laughed. 'But just look at the time, and the potatoes not on! Your dad will be home soon and I'll have to tell him it's not my fault, for you've kept me talking. Now, you run outside like a good girl, and pick me a nice colander full of beans. We don't have time for shelling peas.'

Wandering down the rows of runner beans in her father's neat garden, Millie thought about the day this had been. Of course she had noticed the handsome doctor. Who could fail to do so? Not that looks meant anything. Ted Cooke was good-looking in his own way, but he had proved he could not be trusted. A true heart and a pleasant nature were more important.

Yes, she had warmed to Dr Carson the first time she'd met him. Cheerful and kind he seemed to be, and he must care about other people, or he would not have become a doctor. Yes, he was someone she'd like to get to know better, but there was no point in that, so she might as well put the idea out of her mind.

Miss Julia obviously liked him, and that fact alone definitely put her out of the running. Why would he spare a thought for a little village school-mistress, when he might win the wealthy Julia Pennington? Having such a wife would help him in his career, and that was the way of the world.

Looking up at the sun, shining bright in a clear blue sky, Millie reminded herself of the good life she led. It would be nice to have a loving husband some day, but in the meantime she had a worthwhile job, and plenty of excite-ment to look forward to, what with the Diamond Jubilee celebrations just around the corner.

In addition to the village activities, there would be high jinks up at the Hall, and Ada would come home on her afternoons off to tell them all about the goings-on. There were rumours that titled people were coming to stay, possibly even minor royalty. Mum would love to hear all about the ladies' gowns and the fancy foods made by Mrs Beasley, the cook.

Yes, her life was good, she thought — and, not being blessed with second sight, Millie had no inkling that it couldn't last.

4

Life at Pennington Hall was fast approaching fever pitch, with Blueglass, the butler, issuing orders right and left. Guests had been invited for the Jubilee celebrations, and the house was being cleaned from top to bottom. Having stayed up until past midnight for three nights in a row, he approached Lady Augusta on the subject of extra staff.

'Extra staff, Blueglass? Whatever for?'

'Well, m'lady, with all the guests expected, there's a great deal of work to do. We could use some extra hands, if only to wait at table.'

'And what, pray, did you have in mind?'

'Well, m'lady, one or two extra footmen, I thought, and perhaps a few village women to help with the cleaning.'

Lady Augusta raised her eyebrows.

'Footmen, perhaps, but charwomen? Surely if the maids had been working properly all along, there would not be so very much to do now? They are such a lazy lot. It's your job to keep their noses to the grindstone, Blueglass, so don't come complaining to me if things don't go smoothly. See to it, will you, and let me hear no more about it.'

'Very good, m'lady.'

Outside the door of the morning room, the butler paused, trying to choke down his rage. A lazy lot, were they? Up at dawn and on their feet for eighteen hours, some of them, apart from the meagre two half-hours allotted to meal times.

And it was always his fault if anything went wrong. For two pins he'd look for a different situation, except that his old mother lived not five miles away, and this was a convenient spot, enabling him to visit her now and then.

But in preparation for the guests, bedrooms which had not been occupied for months had to be opened up and the dust sheets removed. Some of them still had the heavy winter curtains hanging at the windows and these had to be taken down and summer chintz draperies substituted. Mats had to be taken outside and thoroughly beaten, and bedding had to be well aired and the beds made up.

All that took time and was extra even to their normal heavy workload.

Out of doors, the gardeners were working overtime, weeding the flower beds and mowing the lawns with the aid of the donkey-driven grass cutter. The tennis court had to be freshly marked out with a hand-pushed chalk machine, and the gravel on the drive had to be carefully raked.

None of that was Blueglass's responsibility, of course, but the complaints of the men when they came indoors at meal times all added to the stress.

Mr James had come home from the university, bringing a friend with him, and the pair of them were constantly demanding attention.

Mrs Beasley had provided porridge, ham, mushrooms, scrambled eggs and kedgeree for breakfast, but Mr James had only demanded to know where the devilled kidneys were.

One night, his friend, one Mr Eustace Rowe-Savage, had taken a glass of whiskey to bed with him and, already three sheets to the wind, had managed to upset it all over himself. Summoned to the room in the middle of the night by the urgent ringing of the bell, Blueglass had to rouse a housemaid from her well-earned sleep to go and change the bedding.

And that wasn't the end of it, either. 'He was very rude to me when I asked him to get up off the bed so I could change the sheets,' she complained later, over breakfast in the servants' hall, 'And when he finally did move he pinched my bottom! I thought this was a respectable house, Mr Blueglass, I really did. If my Mum knew what I'm having to put up with she'd make me give in my notice, I know she would.'

'All right, Susan, that will do. I'll see that it doesn't happen again. Get about your work now, if you please.'

'Yes, Mr Blueglass.'

* * *

'He's a nasty piece of work, that friend of Mr James,' Ada Baker remarked to the under house parlourmaid, when they were attending to the four poster bed in the best guest room. 'Savage by name, Savage by nature, that's what I say. You stay well clear of him, Annie, or you'll be sorry.'

'Mr James is lovely, though, ain't he?' Annie said dreamily. 'I reckon I could fancy him all right.'

'You'll do no such thing, Annie Rivers! You'll land yourself in trouble, you will, if you don't look out. No good can come of servants fancying their masters, my girl, or they'll get taken advantage of. Then where will you be? Out on the road with no reference, and something nasty to look forward to.'

'Aw, Ada, I was only saying . . . '

'Then don't! Now smooth out that sheet at your side and tuck those corners in proper.'

But sadly, it's not only those who go courting trouble who find it, as Ada was shortly to learn.

★　★　★

The long day's work was over at last and the staff congregated in the servants' hall, looking forward to their cocoa. Mrs Beasley was about to put the milk on to boil when she sniffed at the pan suspiciously and put it down with a thump.

'Dratted milk's gone off! Ada, nip across to the dairy, will you, and fetch some fresh? You won't need a lamp; there's a bright moon out tonight. Take Annie with you if you want company.'

But Annie had her shoes off, rubbing her sore feet, and Ada told her not to bother. Having filled her jug with cool milk, she lingered in the yard, breathing in the sweet night air.

Across the courtyard a shadow moved, but she was too busy looking up at the moon to notice. Somewhere far off, an owl hooted, and she wondered if, on such a night her father was somewhere about the estate, looking out for poachers.

'Out for a little walk, are we?'

Ada jumped with shock at the sound of the gruff voice so close in her ear.

'Oh, you did give me a start, sir!' In the gloom she could just make out the face of Eustace Rowe-Savage, although she could not imagine what a guest was doing out in the yard between the dairy and the kitchens.

'I was hoping to meet a pretty little dairy maid,' he said, 'but you'll do just as well, my dear.'

Alarm bells rang in Ada's head. She found herself backed up against the stone wall, with her way blocked by the unsavoury young man. 'Please let me pass, sir. The cook is waiting for this milk, and she'll be very annoyed if I don't get back with it.'

'Mrs Beasley can wait. You and I have a little business to see to.'

'I don't think so!' Ada raised her voice, praying that somebody would hear and come to investigate, but all was quiet. Eustace grabbed her by the shoulders and planted a rough kiss on her mouth. The jug fell from her hands and the milk spilled on the cobbles.

'I'll scream!' Ada gasped, managing to free her mouth from his.

'That would be most unfortunate, when there could be a pleasant interlude between us. Now, where can we go? Perhaps you know of a convenient nearby barn?'

'I'm not going anywhere with you!'

'It's your choice, girl.' He grasped her lace collar and pulled sharply.

As she heard the fabric rip, she lashed out in fear and her fingernails raked down his cheek.

'That does it, you little hell cat!' he

roared, tugging roughly at her skirts.

Desperately she raised her leg and thrust her knee forward with all her strength. Taken off guard he stepped backwards, slipping on the spilt milk. Horrified, Ada saw him sprawled on the ground, and knew she had to get away as fast as possible.

Unfortunately the way back to the kitchen was barred, and she dared not try to step over him. Could she run back to the dairy? But there was no way to lock the door from the inside and she would be cornered there. Should she run to the stables, perhaps, in the hope of rousing someone there? But no, the stablemen all lived out, and would surely be at home by now.

There was only one thing left to do.

Hitching up her skirts she ran to the stile and was up and over in an instant. From there it was a short distance to the main drive and she pelted down it, not daring to look back to see if Eustace was in pursuit.

A cloud had drifted in front of the moon and the sky was black, but Ada knew the way and was able to keep moving. She fell once, but she scarcely felt the pain of her scratched hands.

When she reached the main road she slowed down, pressing a hand into her side and gasping. She had lost one of her soft indoor shoes during her headlong flight, and her foot was starting to bleed, causing her to limp. She still had two miles to go but somehow she would manage to cover the distance, heading for the one place where she knew she would be safe.

She knew this night would bring repercussions, but at the moment she didn't care. All she wanted was to be under her parents' roof, with her mother looking after her.

At that very moment, Fanny Baker was in her kitchen, arguing with her younger daughter. 'Come and put that lamp out. You should be in your bed, asleep. Your dad's been tucked up this past hour, and so should you be.'

They both looked to the door in alarm, as a loud thumping was heard. Before they could move, the door fell open, and Ada stumbled inside in a crumpled heap.

5

'Where has that girl got to? I want my cocoa, and if I don't get to my bed soon I'll fall asleep on my feet.' The cook spoke crossly. It had been a long and tiring day for them all.

'Perhaps the bogey-man got her, Mrs Beasley.' Pansy, the young kitchen maid, was wide-eyed with fear.

'I'll give you bogey-man, my girl! Just for that, you can go and see what's happened to her.'

'Oh, no, Mrs Beasley — please don't make me!'

'I daresay she's gossiping with the dairy maids,' the butler said. The cook looked at him over the top of her spectacles.

'They'll have gone home long ago, surely. You go, then, Mr Blueglass.'

'Oh, very well, but I shall have something to say to that young woman.'

When the butler stepped outside he heard moans coming from a few yards away. Holding his lantern high, he was shocked to see a figure lying on the ground, and on closer inspection he was even more amazed to find that it was Mr Eustace Rowe-Savage.

Racing back to the kitchen door he shouted for John, one of the footmen, who quickly came running.

'It's Mr Rowe-Savage. He seems to have had an accident. Help me up with him, will you? Careful now, boy. You take his legs and I'll carry him under his arms.'

Somehow they managed to bundle the injured man into the house, to the accompaniment of muted shrieks from the female servants. When Mr Eustace was stretched out on the couch in the servants' hall, John was dispatched to fetch James Pennington

'Shouldn't we send for Dr Atwood?' Mrs Beasley whispered. 'He don't look all that good to me.' And indeed, their patient was red-faced, and breathing rather hard.

'We'll leave that for Mr James to decide,' Blueglass said.

'But what on earth happened to him? His face is all scratched, and his arm looks all funny, out of shape, like.'

'We'll have to wait until he comes to, Mrs Beasley, and then he can speak for himself.'

'And where is Ada?' she wailed. 'Surely she didn't have anything to do with this unfortunate business!'

The butler didn't answer, and just then James Pennington arrived, tying his dressing gown cord in a knot as he came.

'What's all this, Blueglass? John here tells me something has happened to old Eustace.'

'Yes, Sir,' Blueglass replied. 'He seems to have met with an accident.'

'Where is he now?'

'We've got him in the servants' hall, sir. I didn't know what to do for the best. Should we sent for Dr Atwood?'

'You'd better let me have a look at him first. He may only be a bit under the weather. He was drinking quite a lot earlier on.'

'Yes, sir.'

'I suggest that the rest of you get off to bed now. You come with me, Blueglass, and you'd better wait, too, John.'

James stared down at his friend with a grim expression on his face. 'He looks as if he's walked into a wall, poor chap. I suppose we ought to get the doc, just in case. First, though, you'd better help me get him up to his bed, and then you can trot off to the village, John.'

'Should I inform Mr Pennington, sir?''

'Heavens, no, Blueglass. No need for that. The next thing we know, Mummy will be disturbed, and we certainly don't want that, do we? Come on now, Eustace old man, up-sa-daisy.'

When the young man had been unceremoniously dumped on his bed, Blueglass was dismissed. He went to his room unwillingly, and although he undressed and went to bed he was unable to fall asleep.

John had taken the trap, and it was about an hour later that he heard it returning. Going to the window to look out, he saw the footman handing the reins to a groom, while another man descended from the conveyance. He was too tall and slim to be old Dr Atwood, so it must be that new young doctor everyone was talking about. Colton, or Carleton, something like that.

'I don't think he's too badly hurt, Mr Pennington,' the doctor said, after a brief examination of his patient. 'A dislocated shoulder, by the feel of things, and a few bumps and bruises. If you'll give me a hand we can soon put that shoulder right. Luckily for him, he's well out of it. How did he come to fall — just staggering about, was he?'

'Managed to slip on some spilt milk, according to Blueglass. Lost his balance, I suppose, being a bit under the weather, though how he happened to come across the milk, I can't imagine.

He was still up when I went to bed, so I really have no idea.'

'Quite. Now, I want you to hold his other arm, just in case he feels anything and fetches me an unlucky one while I'm working.'

His work accomplished, the doctor stepped back and picked up his medical bag. 'I'll call back tomorrow to see how he's doing. Meanwhile, he must stay in bed and be kept quiet, although I doubt he'll feel like moving far. Judging by the fumes on his breath he'll have the mother of all hangovers in the morning.'

'Many thanks, doc. I'll see you out, and arrange for someone to give you a lift back to the village.'

Blueglass watched the trap leaving. *What a to-do*, he thought. *And what had really happened out there?* The broken ewer and the puddle of milk pointed to the fact that Ada had been there, but what had happened to lead to the milk being spilt — and where was she now?

★ ★ ★

Eustace was conscious when James looked in on him in the morning.

'How are you feeling, old chap?'

'Like I've been hit with a ton of bricks. And why is my arm in a sling?'

'You had a fall, and we had to call the medico in. Apparently you had one too many, and down you went.'

Eustace frowned. 'It's coming back to me now. There was a girl, a maid, I think, a stupid little tart. She came at me like a scalded cat.' His hand went up to his cheek. 'Scarred me for life, I shouldn't wonder, and all I wanted was a bit of how's your father.'

'I say, old boy, that's a bit thick, isn't it? Coming here as a guest and groping one of the staff? I don't know what the mater will say if she finds out. She's jolly keen on the girls knowing their place, and all that.'

'It's only a maid, James. They're all fair game, you must admit.'

'Even so, you'd better not come

down to breakfast. I'll have a tray sent up. Those scratches look rather obvious.'

★ ★ ★

Downstairs, Blueglass was anxiously questioning the staff as to the still missing Ada's whereabouts.

'I don't know, I'm sure,' Mrs Beasley said. 'Susan, wasn't she out of bed when you came down to light the boiler?'

'No, Mrs Beasley, and her bed was made up all proper, not left to air like we're supposed to do. I don't think it was slept in.'

'Not slept in! Then where has the naughty girl got to? Oh, I do hope nothing's happened to her!'

'I told you it was the bogey-man,' Pansy quavered.

'And I told you not to be so silly, my girl.'

'But if that Mister Eustace was attacked, then somebody bad must have been out there, and since Ada's missing, he must have got her, too. She could be lying out there somewhere, dead as a doornail.' The kitchen maid broke down and sobbed loudly.

'Now you just stop that this instant and get busy making fresh toast. They'll be asking for it upstairs, and now I have to lay a tray for that Mr Eustace as well. Pull yourself together, my girl, unless you want to feel the weight of my hand!'

Blueglass, meanwhile, was trying to decide what to do. While he had hoped to keep quiet about the events of the night before, it was obvious that he had to speak to the master of the Hall now.

'Can I have a word with you, sir?'

'Yes, Blueglass, what is it?'

'It's Ada, sir, the head house parlour maid.'

'Yes, yes, what about her, man? Anything to do with the maids should be referred to my wife.'

'Yes, sir, I know, but I didn't want to bother Lady Augusta with this. You see, the girl went out to the dairy last night but has not returned, nor is she to be found this morning.'

'Dallying with some young man, I suppose. You know that we don't permit followers, Blueglass.'

'I know, sir, but that's not all. We found the milk spilled on the ground near the door, with no sign of the girl. Your son's college friend apparently slipped on it, and had rather a bad fall. We had to summon the doctor.'

'Rowe-Savage? Well, you did quite right, of course. As for the girl, when she does turn up, send her straight to me. We cannot have this kind of thing going on in the house, especially not at the moment, when we've so much on our plates with the Diamond Jubilee celebrations.'

'No, sir. Very well, sir.' Blueglass retreated, bowing slightly.

6

Fanny stood with her hand to her mouth, while Millie ran to help her sister, half carrying her into the room. 'What on earth has happened to you, Ada? Just look at the state you're in.'

Fanny came forward to support her elder daughter, guiding her to a chair nearest to the range. Ada was indeed a sight, with her uniform dress torn and muddied where she'd fallen on the road, and her hair awry. Her face was dirty and tear-stained.

'Oh, your poor foot!' Fanny cried. 'You're torn to bits, child. And where is your shoe? Lost it, have you?'

Ada shook her head wordlessly.

'And why are you here, at this time of night? This in't your half day, is it? Talk to me, Ada! Tell me what's happened!'

'I think she's too upset,' Millie suggested. 'Let me help you up to bed,

Ada, and when you've got settled I'll bring you a nice cup of tea, all right?'

'She'll have to bathe that foot first,' Fanny said, recovering her wits. 'We don't want that going septic. Perhaps we should call the doctor, just to make sure she's all right. She may have been attacked.'

'I don't want the doctor,' Ada croaked. 'I'll be all right in the morning.'

'I certainly hope you will, child, but in the meantime, if you won't have the doctor, I'm going to rouse your father. You stay there and soak your foot.'

'Don't fetch Dad!'

'Don't you tell me what to do, my girl. He's your father, and he has a right to know what's going on under his roof.'

Abel Baker made his way down the stairs, rubbing his eyes. He wore a striped nightshirt, and a cotton nightcap which almost covered his bushy eyebrows. He stopped short when he saw Ada, sitting there with her feet in the preserving pan.

'Your mother tells me you've been attacked, girl. Is that right?'

Ada nodded.

'Who was he? I'll kill the rotten devil!' His eyes went to the shotgun, propped up in the corner, and Ada knew he meant what he said.

'It's all right, Dad. He didn't do me any harm. I got him with my knee in the you-know-whats.'

'Ada!' Fanny was shocked to the core. 'What sort of talk is that? How would you even think of such a thing, and you a well brought up girl!'

'It's all right, Mum. I've got brothers, so I do know a thing or two. Before he went to Canada, our Jack told me what to do if anything like this ever happened to me.'

'But if you managed to get the better of the boy, why did you run off? What are you doing here at this time of night, and dressed in your indoor uniform, too?'

'I was scared, Dad. It wasn't just

some village boy. His name is Mr Eustace Rowe-Savage, and he's a college friend of Mr James.'

'And you didn't encourage him in any way? You know I've always warned you against getting involved with the gentry.'

'No, Dad. Cook sent me to the dairy for milk, and he must have been waiting in the shadows for some poor girl to come along. Then he pounced, and I tried to talk my way out of it, but it didn't do any good.'

'So that was when you . . . er . . . '

'Yes, but when he grabbed me I dropped the milk jug, and the stuff went everywhere, and then he slipped on it and fell down. I was afraid he'd done himself an injury, and I'd get the blame. I couldn't get past him to get back inside, and I thought he'd come after me, so I just ran. He was drunk as a lord, Dad. I wasn't sure I could fend him off a second time.'

'Don't you worry, gal. He won't have hurt himself, a young fellow like that.

Drunks seldom do.'

'I'm sure to get turned off without a reference, Dad.' A big tear rolled down Ada's cheek. 'We're not allowed to leave the house without permission, you know that.'

'We'll see about that, my girl! I'll be up at the Hall first thing in the morning, and if anyone gets turfed out it will be that Savage, or whatever his name is. Now, I'm going back to my bed, and we'll deal with this tomorrow.'

* * *

When morning came, Fanny was the first one up. Her first task was to remove Abel's shotgun before he could get hold of it. While she was quite sure that he'd never point it at anyone — poachers excepted — Basil Pennington wouldn't think much of his gamekeeper bringing a possibly loaded weapon into the house, frightening the women. Besides, in the heat of the moment it might go off accidentally.

When Abel clattered downstairs, tying a spotted handkerchief round his neck as he came, Fanny was ready to say her piece.

'I do hope you've changed your mind about going up to the Hall,' she began at once.

'Changed my mind? Why on earth would I do that? Ada has been hurt and terrified, and I'm the girl's father. It's my job to protect her. Are you suggesting we send her back up there alone to face the music?'

'Then what do you mean to do?'

'I don't know yet. I'll see how the land lies when I get there.'

That was what Fanny was afraid of. Her husband was a good man, usually slow to anger, but if anything did set him off, you had better watch out. What if he gave Eustace Rowe-Savage a good thumping, as he would any village youth who had behaved in similar fashion? The Penningtons were likely to bring the law down on him.

Or suppose he gave Basil Pennington

a piece of his mind, and got himself the sack? He might never get another permanent job again. What was more, they'd be left without a roof over their heads, for this was a tied cottage, one that went with the job.

It had been Fanny's home for almost thirty years, and, simple though it was, she couldn't bear the thought of leaving it. How would they manage, doomed to tramp the roads in search of odd jobs, sleeping in barns and under hedges? She said as much to Abel.

'A man has to act according to his principles,' he told her, which was scant consolation. Fortunately Millie came down the stairs at this moment, interrupting the tense moment.

'I want you to leave a few minutes early this morning, Millie,' he told her.

'Yes, Dad. Why's that, then?'

'You'll have to go and leave word for the doctor to call to see our Ada when he's on his rounds.'

'Which doctor, Dad?'

'I don't care. I want to be able to tell

them up there that she's too badly off to report for work. It might buy her some time.'

Millie nodded. 'Yes, Dad. I meant to set off early in any case, so I can look in on Miss Powell.'

'Give the old girl my regards, then.'

'I will, Dad,' Millie replied.

'Have you looked in on Ada yet this morning?' her mother asked anxiously. 'How is she?'

'She was still asleep when I came down.'

'And sleep is just what she needs,' Fanny said. 'There's nothing like it for healing body and mind.' She turned to her husband. 'Look, Abel, why go up to the Hall this morning? Why don't you wait until the doctor's been and we've heard what he has to say?' She was still hoping to deter him from walking into trouble.

He frowned. 'Are you trying to tell me my own business, woman? As head of this family it's my job to protect everyone in it, and that's just what I intend to do.'

'Do you want anything from the shop, Mum?' Millie wanted to interrupt this conversation before it descended into a full-blown row. There was no point in getting Dad all worked up before he even arrived at the Hall.

'What did you say, Millie?' Fanny asked distractedly.

'I wondered if you need me to pick up anything from the shop on my way home. I thought with Ada coming home unexpectedly you might need to get in a few extras.'

'No, no, dear, I'm all right, and anyway, it wouldn't surprise me if Mrs Beasley handed your dad a few treats to bring home. She's always had a soft spot for Abel, and when she hears what's happened to poor Ada she'll want to do what she can, I feel sure.'

'That's if I even get past the door,' Abel snapped. 'Who knows what that young pup has told them all. He'll not want to put himself in the wrong, will he? That's one reason why I want the doctor brought to Ada, so he'll be able to speak for her if necessary.'

Grunting as he pulled on his knee boots, Abel Baker readied himself for action. In his mind he was no longer a country gamekeeper, fighting against poachers and marauding foxes. One of his womenfolk had been wronged, and he was Saint George, off to tackle the dragon.

Fanny noticed the look in his eye and bit her lip. The next few hours would decide their future and she only hoped he was equal to the challenge.

The door banged shut behind him and he was gone.

Sighing, Fanny climbed the stairs to look in on poor Ada.

★   ★   ★

Millie ran all the way to the village, stopping only once when she had a stitch in her side. When she arrived at The Firs, which was never referred to as anything other than 'the doctor's house', she was gasping and panting and had to take a moment to compose herself before ringing the bell.

The door was thrown open at once and to add to her confusion, it was not the housekeeper who stood there, but young Dr Carson.

'Hello, Miss Baker. You're an early bird! All is well with Miss Powell, I trust?' he asked brightly.

'Oh, yes. That is, I hope so, but I haven't seen her yet this morning. It's my sister who needs a doctor. My mother — that is, my father — wants Dr Atwood to call on her.'

'You'd better come in and sit down for a moment. You're all out of breath.' Pretending not to notice her confusion, he stood aside to let her in. She sank down on a convenient chair, trying to slow her breathing.

'Now then, what seems to be the matter? Has she a fever?'

'Oh, no, I don't think so. She ran all the way home from the Hall last night and she lost a shoe on the way. Her foot is quite badly cut.'

'It sounds to me as if she was in a bit of a hurry.'

Millie hesitated. Ada wouldn't thank her for talking about what had happened, but this was a doctor, and he'd get to know sooner or later. 'Something bad happened to her,' she said at last. 'She was attacked, although she managed to fight the man off. She felt she had to come home to Mum and Dad.'

'I see.' Was this something to do with that incident up at the Hall, he wondered? Naturally, medical ethics prohibited him from discussing his night-time visit to attend James Pennington's university friend, but this bore looking into. 'Don't worry, Miss Baker. I'll call to see to your sister this morning. We'll soon have her put right.'

'Oh, but your surgery . . . '

'It's Dr Atwood's turn to take surgery. I was just about to set off on my rounds, which is why I opened the door so quickly — you caught me just in time before I left.'

Having given him directions to the

gamekeeper's cottage, Millie made her way to the schoolhouse, where she found Miss Powell hopping about valiantly. The pair were soon busily discussing the plans for the school day.

* ★ *

It suited Edwin Carson very well to make the Baker home his first stop on his day's rounds.

Fanny greeted him anxiously. 'I'm so glad you've come, Doctor! My poor girl came home last night in a terrible state. She somehow managed to step on a piece of broken glass, and she must be in such pain with that foot. And she had a terrible shock — '

'I'll see the patient now,' Edwin said, interrupting her breathless flow of talk. The poor woman seemed so upset that she might need medical assistance herself as well.

Fanny led the way up the stairs, opening the door onto a tiny room containing two beds. It was tucked underneath the roof, so that the sloping ceiling came to down almost to the floor. 'Here's the doctor to see you, dear,' she said.

Ada sat up, raking her fingers through her hair to smooth it down. 'Oh, Mum, you might have warned me. I haven't even washed my face yet.'

'Of course you haven't, dear. You've been sleeping until now.'

'I'll see that foot before you do anything else, anyway,' Edwin said. Ada winced as he probed the torn flesh. 'Nothing that can't be mended, Miss Baker,' he said, then turning to Fanny, he added, 'See that she bathes this three times a day, in warm water with Epsom salts added.'

'Yes, Doctor.'

'I can't do that!' Ada grumbled. 'I've got to get back to work before I lose my place. That's if I still have a job, after last night.'

'If you attempt to walk on that foot before it's properly healed and it turns septic, you could lose it altogether, never mind your job. And what's all this about last night? Did something happen to you?'

Hesitantly, Ada told her story, with her mother chipping in now and then with expressions of woe.

'I'm so afraid I'll lose my job, Doctor,' she said at last. 'I came home last night without permission, and I know people have been sacked for less.'

'You can hardly be blamed for running away from an attacker,' Edwin Carson said incredulously.

'But that's not all, Doctor. I had to fight him off, you see, and he fell over. The last I saw of him he was lying on the ground. I kept expecting him to catch up with me, but he didn't, so he must have been badly hurt when he fell. He might even be dead!' Ada's eyes were wide with terror.

'I can assure you that the young man is very much alive, although slightly the worse for wear.'

'You've seen him, Doctor?' Fanny chipped in.

'As it happens, I was called to attend to him last night.'

Ada sank back on the pillows, feeling weak with relief. 'I'll still be in trouble, though, I know it. Scratching and pummelling a friend of Mr James! The Pennington family won't like that.'

Fanny turned to Dr Carson, her face working with distress. 'Doctor, I know I shouldn't ask, but can't you say that our Ada is too ill to return to work? If I could only keep her here until all the fuss dies down a bit, it might be for the best.' Wringing her hands, she continued, 'I'm sure she'll still get the sack, but with any luck they won't turn her out without a reference. At least then she'll be able to go elsewhere to get a job. Otherwise she's finished, an unmarried woman without work.'

'Calm yourself, Mrs Baker, do. Of course I'll give her a chit to say she has to stay off work. No, don't thank me,' he added, quick to evade Mrs Baker's profuse gratitude. 'It's no word of a lie, for that foot needs proper care. And I'll have a tonic made up for the pair of you. You look as though you could do with one yourself, Mrs Baker.'

*   *   *

Edwin Carson went on his way to his next patient, a little girl who had come out in spots. As he pedalled on he pondered over what he had just heard. It was a hard world where a poor girl could lose her livelihood merely for fending off an attacker. He hoped that she was mistaken in what she expected the Penningtons' reaction would be.

He had taken an instant dislike to the drunken man he'd been called out to attend to last night. Even though the brute was only semi-conscious at the time, Edwin had been treated to a volley of filthy words.

He had not looked forward to paying a return call today, but now it would give him the opportunity of finding out how the land lay. If it proved to be necessary for him to come to Ada's defence at a later date, it would be as well to have all the facts in his possession.

'Good morning, Dr Carson!' a voice called out.

Deep in thought, he had been only half aware of the approaching horse, and now he swung round at the sound of Julia Pennington's voice.

She was riding a fine bay mare, side-saddle of course, and dressed like a fashion plate. His eyes took in her fine blue riding habit and the little hat, complete with veil, perched on her glossy hair.

'You're out early, Miss Pennington.'

'I didn't sleep well, so I thought I might as well come out for a good gallop, to blow away the cobwebs.'

'An excellent idea.'

'My maid tells me you were at the Hall last night. You might have dropped by to say hello.'

'It was far too late, Miss Pennington, and in any case it wasn't a social call,' Edwin replied politely.

'I know. I heard something about it. That friend of Jamie's got drunk and had a fall or something, serves him right. Now perhaps Mama will stop thinking of him as a possible suitor for me.'

'Is that why he's here?' Edwin asked without thinking. 'I'm sorry, Miss Pennington; I should not have asked such an impertinent question.'

'Oh, that's quite all right. I'm not interested in him, anyway. He's much too young and stupid.'

'Then why . . . ?'

'Oh, he's third cousin to a Duke or something. But no, he wasn't brought here to be dangled in front of my nose. He rooms with my brother at college, and Jamie brought him home to join in the Jubilee celebrations. Apparently he's a good cricketer, demon bowler or something, and they need him on their team for the big match against the other villages.' She bestowed a beatific smile on Edwin. 'Do you play cricket, Dr Carson?'

'When I have time.'

'Oh, good. I'll tell Daddy, and I'm sure they'll rope you in. I can give you my handkerchief to wear, to bring you luck — like those ladies in olden days when men went jousting.'

'I'm afraid I wouldn't be very reliable, Miss Pennington. I'm likely to be called away at any moment to attend to a patient.'

'Rubbish!' she scoffed. 'Everyone will be there, watching the match, and they'll need a doctor on the spot, in case someone gets hit on the head with the ball. Now don't forget what I said. You can be my swain, and I shall be your lady.'

And with that, she turned her horse's head, and pressed the animal into a canter without another word.

Edwin Carson watched her go. He told himself that Miss Julia Pennington bore careful watching — if he ever gave in to her blandishments he had better take care, for he suspected that she gobbled up young men as the fancy took her, only to spit them out again when she had tired of them. All very well for her, but not for the men, especially if any of them took her seriously.

As for himself, although he was flattered to think that she found him worthy of her attentions, he had better watch his step. He had a position to keep up here, and as a doctor he must avoid any whiff of scandal.

7

'A man's come!' Pansy called back over her shoulder excitedly as she stood on the doorstep of the kitchens.

'Well don't keep him standing on the doorstep, then!' Mrs Beasley said. 'Bring him inside!' She stared at Abel in surprise. 'Mr Baker! I hope you haven't come looking for your Ada, for we haven't seen hide nor hair of her since last night.'

'It's answers I'm looking for,' Abel said, his expression grim. 'Where is Mr Blueglass?'

'Up in the morning room. He was rung for, but I daresay he'll be back in a minute. There's been a real old to-do here. Mr Eustace, a guest in the house, was attacked last night, and they had to fetch the doctor to him.'

'I'll give him attacked, the young pup! It's our Ada who was attacked, and I'm only thankful she managed to fight him off before any harm was done.'

'Never!' Mrs Beasley gasped.

'Yes, indeed. My wife is keeping her in bed this morning, and there she'll stay until the doctor's been to see to her. On top of everything else, she's badly shocked.'

'I have to sit down,' the cook murmured, pressing her hand to her chest. 'I've come over all queer. You sit down as well, Mr Baker, and Pansy will pour you a cup of tea. There's some made fresh in the pot.'

'I don't mind if I do, Mrs Beasley.'

'You said 'on top of everything else.' What does that mean, exactly?'

'The poor girl ran home barefoot nearly all the way and she's cut to pieces. She won't be able to walk properly for a good while, if ever.'

'Tut, tut! Oh, here comes Mr Blueglass now.'

Abel stood up to face the butler, repeating his tale. Blueglass recognised an irate father when he saw one. 'I'm sorry to hear this, Mr Baker, and poor Ada has my sympathy, you may be sure. It's coming to something when one of the staff should come to harm in this house. However, this latest development must be reported to Mr Pennington. He already knows of Mr Rowe-Savage's accident, and he's none too pleased about it.'

'Accident!' Abel bellowed. 'It was no accident!'

'Yes. Apparently the young chap was pushed by Ada, and he slipped in a puddle of milk. He was badly shaken up, and his shoulder was dislocated.'

'It's too bad he didn't break his neck, then,' Abel retorted sharply.

'We must be thankful that nothing of the kind occurred, Mr Baker, or the girl might hang for it. Now, if you'll excuse me, I must go and inform the master that Ada has been found.'

'Oh, no, you don't! I have a thing or two to say to Mr Pennington, and I won't leave here until I've said my piece!'

'Oh, do be careful!' Mrs Beasley cried. 'You know what his temper's like. He's just as likely to sack you on the spot, and you don't want that!'

'You sound like my wife, Mrs Beasley, but this is a matter of principle. If a man can't stand up for his daughter, then it's a sorry thing.'

Having been announced by Blue-glass, Abel found himself standing, cap in hand, on a thick Turkish carpet, the price of which would have kept his family for several years. He waited for his employer to speak.

'A guest in this house has been hurt, Baker, and he accuses your daughter of having flown at him like a wild thing, after which she apparently ran off into the night. He's talking about pressing charges, Baker, and I'm not sure I don't agree with him. As it is, the very least I can do under the circumstances is to dismiss her from my service. I trust you understand.'

Abel took a deep breath. 'Oh, I understand, all right, sir. I thought this a respectable house, not one where the young female servants have to fight for their honour! That young pup tried to interfere with my daughter and what he needs is a good thrashing! And that's what he'll get if I ever manage to lay my hands on him.'

'Now, Baker, none of that! Do you want to find yourself in gaol?'

'Then I hope he'll soon be on his way back to wherever it is he came from. As for Ada getting the sack, that's the usual thing with the gentry, isn't it? Some poor girl gets taken advantage of and when she finds herself in the family way she's thrown out. 'Getting scarlet fever', they call it, don't they? And with no reference, she can never get another job so she ends up in the gutter. And what happens to the chap? Nothing at all, he gets off scot-free, sowing his wild oats, that's what they say, isn't it?' He barely stopped long enough to take a breath.

'Well, my daughter has had a narrow escape, and never mind the sack, I wouldn't let her spend another day under this roof. But I'll expect you to provide her with a good reference, all the same. Thanks to that fellow upstairs she'll have to leave the village to find other employment, and what her poor mother will say to that, I cannot think!'

Having run out of steam, Abel stood trembling with anger, waiting for his own dismissal to come.

Basil Pennington walked over to the window and stood looking out, his hands clasped behind his back.

'Just think if it was Miss Julia,' Abel added softly.

'What's that? How dare you, Baker! There's absolutely no need to bring my family into this!' But before anything more could be said the door flew open, and Miss Julia herself bounced in.

'Sorry, Papa! I didn't know anyone else was here.'

'It's all right, Julia. Baker was just leaving. Off you go about your business, Baker. You've wasted enough time already this morning.'

Dismissed, Abel had no choice but to leave.

'Whew, you came on a bit strong, didn't you?' Blueglass muttered, as they made their way back to the basement. 'Lucky for you Miss Julia turned up when she did. I thought the old man was about to burst when you brought her name into it.'

'Don't tell me he wouldn't take a horse whip to anyone who laid hands on his darling daughter. It's one rule for the gentry and another for you and me, Mr Blueglass, and you know it.'

'And you've only now found that out?' The butler's smile did not reach his eyes. 'What will you do next, then?'

'Get to work, I s'pose.' Abel shrugged. 'No point putting his back up any more than I already have.'

'And Ada?'

'I meant what I said, Mr Blueglass. No matter what the master decides, I'm not letting her come back here,' Abel said firmly. 'Not while that Savage chap is still around.'

'She'll be missed, Mr Baker.'

'Thank you, Mr Blueglass. I'll tell her you said so.'

* * *

Trudging down the long drive to the main road, Abel met a young man on a bicycle, who had just come through the tall wrought-iron gates and was obviously bound for the house. For a brief moment he wondered if this was Savage-Rowe, but Blueglass had said something about the chap being upstairs in bed, being waited on hand and foot by the maids who, Abel was certain, had better things to do.

Abel touched his cap as the newcomer sped by, calling out a cheerful 'Good morning!'

Edwin Carson, on his way to the Hall, guessed that he had just greeted Ada's father. Wearing a Norfolk jacket, cord britches and polished gaiters, the man was obviously a gamekeeper or estate manager. Most farm labourers

91

were much more shabbily dressed.

It took the doctor some time to cycle on up the long drive to the Hall and when he was finally shown into the room, he found his patient sprawled on a couch, smoking a cigar.

'You're up and about, I see,' he observed.

'Who the devil are you?'

'I'm Dr Carson. I was called last night, when you had your accident.' He was met with a blank look and added, 'You don't remember?'

'I remember some little skivvy coming at me like a scalded cat. Just look at my face! I shan't be able to go out in public for weeks.'

'That little skivvy, as you call her, won't be appearing in public for some time to come. By the way,' Edwin said firmly, turning to James Pennington, who was hovering uselessly in the background, 'here is a chit to affirm that the girl won't be returning to work until her injuries are fully healed. That could take some time.'

'Injuries!' Eustace scoffed. 'I didn't touch her, unless you count a little kiss, and what's wrong with that, eh?'

'You were drunk, man!' Dr Carson raged. 'I doubt you have any recollection of what you did. Of course, the drink provides you with the perfect excuse, doesn't it? And to judge by the smell on your breath, you've been hitting the bottle already this morning.' His glance took in the whisky decanter and half-filled glass on the side table.

'Get out of here! I didn't send for you, and I don't need you. Get out of here, I say!'

'Better do as he says, old chap,' James Pennington said quietly. 'He's not quite himself this morning.'

'I should say he's very much himself,' Edwin replied, with a look of distaste at the young man on the couch. 'If he's any friend of yours I suggest you point out the error of his ways, before it's too late. He's likely to get gut rot before he's very much older.'

'I don't think he'll listen to me,'

James bleated. 'I honestly didn't think he was like this, or I'd never have invited him here.'

Fuming, Edwin followed Blueglass to the door and out of the Hall. He was quite sure that he'd never see a fee for this visit.

8

The next two weeks were busy ones as a horde of guests descended on the Hall. The maids were kept busy running up and down with all the tasks that affect a household routine when visitors are present. Hot water for baths, carried up flights of stairs in copper jugs. Chamber pots to empty, rooms to clean. At least it was summer and there were no fires to light or endless scuttles of coal to carry.

Mrs Beasley was in her element, preparing sumptuous meals, and complaining all the while. 'All them extra people! I don't know why they want to come here,' she grumbled. 'Why can't they all stay up in London, with all the goings-on there? I couldn't have more to do if we were having a wedding right here in the Hall!'

The pace of life had accelerated at

the village school as well, as the day of the celebrations drew near. The children were in a fever of excitement, which made learning difficult. All they could think about was the funfair which was being set up in the field behind the school. A dozen times a day they reminded Millie of the joys to come. In addition to a roundabout, with garishly painted horses, there were to be swing boats and coconut shies, to name only a few of the attractions.

The problem was that most of them had very little money to spend, so how were they supposed to decide which to choose? Millie took no notice, knowing that anticipation was part of the fun, as was wandering around the fair, taking in all the sights. In any case, most parents would probably try to shell out a penny or two for their youngsters when the time came.

The Penningtons' guests were highly visible in the village. Either they were out riding, or they were wandering about, commenting unfavourably on everything they saw.

'Dunno why they can't stay up at the house where they belongs,' one old man grumbled, in Fanny's hearing. 'Galloping about on they great horses! Almost ran down my grandchild, they did, when he put his nose outside his own gate! If he hadn't taken fright and run to his mother, he could be dead as a doornail now.'

As for Millie, she was most annoyed when two ladies opened the door of the school and glanced inside, not bothering to even explain their presence. 'How quaint!' one of them said in a piercing voice, before retreating.

So it was with no small amount of relief that the villagers learned that the entire Pennington family and their guests had gone to London, to view the Jubilee procession.

This, of course, was just one of the many special events planned for the celebrations, but it was bound to be a day to remember. Dignitaries were arriving from all over the Empire and, as Lady Augusta said, they would never see the like again, or at least not in their lifetime.

'Except for the funeral,' Basil Pennington remarked. 'The old girl can't live forever, can she? Before we know it all these European royals and foreign potentates will be back here, for another sort of procession.'

'Basil! What a thing to say! I'm going to London even if you won't come. My cousin Agatha has invited us to her town house, overlooking the procession route. We'll see everything in comfort and she's promised us champagne and strawberries. I'm so looking forward to it. I don't get much of a life, tucked away here in the country, and neither does poor Julia. Besides, I have no wish to offend Agatha, especially when she has agreed to sponsor Julia for her season next year.'

'Oh, I suppose I'll have to come, if only to get rid of young Rowe-Savage. He'll have no excuse for staying on if we take James to London with us.'

'I thought you said you'd had a word with James, telling him to cut the boy's visit short?'

'He tried, apparently, but the boy refused to budge. Said he wasn't well enough to travel, or some such tomfoolery.'

'How very odd. I trust you'll see to it that he leaves for London when we do. Really, Basil, I don't know what James sees in that young man. He hasn't displayed much judgement there.'

'I'll have a word with the boy myself, though it's a bit much, giving a guest his marching orders. Not quite the gentlemanly thing to do, what?'

Augusta gave a small shrug. 'He certainly doesn't seem to know how a gentleman should behave in another man's house. I will not have visitors under this roof upsetting my staff. Mind you, I still feel that the girl must have led him on in some way. You know how these village girls are.'

'I know that I've come close to losing a good gamekeeper over this.'

'Don't be silly, dear. Servants are ten a penny. Go up and see the boy now, before you change your mind. I want to enjoy myself in London, not worry about what might be happening here while we're gone.'

* * *

And so Eustace Rowe-Savage was dispatched back to his home in Banbury, accompanied to the railway station by an indignant Blueglass.

'There is absolutely no need for you to come inside,' Eustace said loftily, when they reached the station. 'I'm not a felon, to have you clamped to my side, and I'm quite capable of making the journey alone.'

'Mr Pennington instructed me to see you on to the train, sir.'

'And you're afraid that if you let me out of your sight I just might double back, and turn up at the Hall again, like a bad penny.'

'Nothing of the sort, sir,' Blueglass

said, although secretly he was indeed afraid of that very thing. When the train arrived and the boy was safely aboard, Blueglass remained on the platform, determined not to leave until the train had pulled out and disappeared from view.

★　★　★

Back at the Hall, meanwhile, Miss Julia was in the middle of an argument with her mother.

'Really, Julia! I despair of you sometimes, I really do!' Lady Augusta cried in exasperation.

'Oh, Mama, really! What a to-do, just because I said I'd like to invite Edwin to come to London with us!'

'That is exactly what I mean, child. Edwin, as you call him, is a doctor, and not even our own doctor, at that. Dr Atwood has always been our doctor and it's simply not suitable for — '

'I know, Mama,' Julia interrupted. 'That's why I can see Edwin, as a friend, since I'm not his patient.'

'Now look here, Julia. When I was young, doctors were not entertained in one's house. In fact, when they did call, they knew their place and went to the tradesman's entrance.'

'Queen Anne is dead, Mama,' Julia muttered.

'There is no need for insolence, child. And at least young Dr Carter knows how to behave. When you so far forgot yourself as to invite him to our little sherry party, of all things, he did not come, did he?'

'That's because he had to see a patient, Mama.'

'So he told you. As I have said to you before, a lady cannot afford to make any unfortunate liaisons, and there must not be even a whiff of scandal which might stop you from being presented at Court next year. Do try to pull yourself together, darling!'

Lady Augusta sighed impatiently. 'When you have your London Season you'll meet plenty of suitable young men of your own class and you'll be able to have your pick of those. Indeed, I see no reason why you shouldn't be able to catch a duke's son.'

'I intend to marry for love,' Julia retorted loftily.

'That was my mistake,' Lady Augusta said. 'And see where it got me.'

Julia shrugged. Her mother was an earl's daughter who had married plain Mr Pennington. Although she was able to keep her own title, she had always resented the fact that Basil did not have one to match. However, she had nothing else to complain about. A fine house and grounds, servants galore, and plenty of money to go with it.

As for Dr Edwin Carson, surely he was good enough for a little dalliance, for what else was there to do in Pennington Parva? Empty-headed Julia might be, but even she wouldn't be foolish enough to tie herself down as a doctor's wife, living in a pokey little house with a man who was out and about day and night, attending to the peasants. She supposed that she would have to marry some witless aristocrat sooner or later, but in the meantime she meant to have a little fun.

The house party earlier had been a severe disappointment to her. Most of the guests had been older people, friends or relations of her parents — or worse, unmarried daughters whom Julia had been forced to entertain.

The only man anywhere near her age had been the dreadful Eustace Rowe-Savage, that boorish friend of her brother James. The man couldn't even hold his drink and he was obviously no gentleman.

What had really transpired between Eustace and the maid, Ada? According to James, the girl had attacked his friend, all because the poor chap had given her a kiss in passing.

On the other hand Susan, one of the other maids, had told Julia a highly coloured tale of Ada's father storming up to the house, demanding justice. She should have been dismissed for her unseemly behaviour but Baker had got in first, refusing to let the girl come back to face the music.

'What do they say about it downstairs?' Julia had asked Susan. 'After all, she's behaved very badly and she's fortunate that Mr Rowe-Savage hasn't insisted upon pressing charges.'

'Begging your pardon, Miss, but they're all on her side,' Susan replied.

'Really? How strange.'

'Yes, Miss, but they think he was the one as done wrong — and if he can get away with it, there's none of us safe.'

'Oh, well, he's gone now, and I don't think he'll be invited here again. It's been a storm in a tea cup, wouldn't you say?'

'I don't know, Miss, I'm sure.'

9

Millie was nearing home when she was almost knocked down by a cyclist, who came flying around the corner. She stepped back just in time, recognising Ted Cooke. He gave her a cheerful wave and pedalled on. Fuming, she ran the last few steps home to the gamekeeper's cottage.

'Hello, love. Had a good day at school, did you?' Fanny asked.

'Hello, Mum. What was that Ted Cooke doing here? I hope you didn't let him over the doorstep.'

'He's been coming to see your sister. Bringing flowers and that. I couldn't very well send him off with a flea in his ear now, could I?'

'You didn't let him see our Ada!' Millie gasped.

'Give me credit for a bit of sense, lass. I could hardly take him upstairs, with her in bed. That wouldn't do much for her reputation, even with me as chaperone. In any case, if anyone is to send him on his way, that's up to Ada, don't you think?'

'We'll see about that!' Dropping her bag of school supplies, Millie ran up the stairs, bursting into the bedroom she shared with her sister. Ada was sitting on the edge of the bed, with her feet in a basin of warm water and Epsom salts. A pretty vase stood on the bedside table, holding an assortment of cottage garden flowers.

'I suppose that weasel Ted Cooke brought you those!' Millie snapped.

'Yes, he did, actually. You don't mind, do you?'

'Not for myself,' Millie said, sitting down heavily on the edge of the bed beside Ada. 'I couldn't care less about that idiot. It's you I'm worried about.'

'No harm in getting a few flowers, is there?'

'Oh, Ada! You know what I mean. He broke your heart once — don't let it happen again. And it could have caused even more trouble,' Millie went on. 'If you hadn't found out in time what he was up to.'

'I haven't even spoken to him yet,' Ada replied, slightly defensively. 'Perhaps he'll get tired of cycling over here every day, for it's a long way from the mill. But never mind about him.' Ada smiled broadly. 'I had a visitor today — Susan from the Hall. It's her afternoon off and she came to bring me a jam sponge Mrs Beasley baked for me.'

'Oh, yes?' Millie's face relaxed somewhat.

'And of course she brought me all the news. The Penningtons and their guests have all gone up to London to see the Jubilee procession and that beastly Eustace has been given his marching orders.'

'I should think so, too. Did she say anything else? Are the Penningtons going to take you back when your foot is mended?'

'She didn't mention that, but the

Penningtons are hardly likely to fall on my neck, are they? Never mind Ted; any decent people would have been on the doorstep with flowers long since. But I'm only a servant, not worth considering. I wouldn't go back there if they forked out a year's wages — and Dad agrees with me.'

'Then what will you do?'

'Once I'm on my feet again, I can't be sponging on Mum and Dad.'

'But where on earth will you go? There's nobody else hereabouts that has servants, except for the doctors, and they already have someone. You'll have to leave the village, and go among strangers.'

'I think I've had enough of service in any case, and I don't fancy field work. P'raps I'll go to Gloucester and get a proper job there. I rather fancy working in a sweet shop.'

'I doubt you'd be able to keep yourself on a shop assistant's wages. I suppose you could get a cheap bed-sitter somewhere, but what kind of life will that be?' Millie asked, full of concern. 'After you pay the rent, you'll have nothing left over.'

'What else is there for a woman? I don't fancy nursing, not after emptying all those beastly chamber pots at the Hall. The only other road open to the likes of me is marriage . . . '

'Don't tell me you're thinking of marrying Ted!' Millie was aghast. Her sister looked at her sadly.

'We haven't all had your chances, Millie. You can have your teaching job for life, if you want it. Play your cards right and you could get the post of headmistress when Miss Powell retires, be able to stay here in the village, with a house thrown in. You'll be on hand to take care of Mum and Dad in their old age, if I'm out of the picture.'

'I doubt the governors would appoint me — certainly not at my age and with my level of experience.'

'That's all in the future, isn't it? Meanwhile, I have to look out for myself.'

Fanny's voice wafted up from the kitchen. 'Are you going to stay up there all night, our Millie? I need a hand with these spuds!'

'Coming, Mum.' Millie hastened downstairs, but her mind was in turmoil.

'What on earth is the matter with you, gal?' Fanny asked. 'You look like you lost sixpence and found a penny.'

'Oh, Mum — I'm worried about our Ada.'

'I don't see why. That foot of hers is coming along nicely, and according to young Susan them Penningtons are off up to London, and nothing said about that Savage chap causing more trouble.'

'But it's Ted, Mum. She may be thinking about marrying him, to save her going back into service. You know what he's like. She'll never be able to trust him. She'll wed him, and things will rub along for a while, then some day on his travels he'll spot a pretty face, and he'll fall from grace again.'

Fanny laughed. 'I've no way of

knowing what's in Ada's mind, but time to worry about that when young Ted manages to have a word with her. For all I know he's coming here because he's got a guilty conscience. That don't mean he's about to propose marriage again.'

'But you said he's been showing up every day.'

'So has the young Dr Carson, but that don't mean he's sweet on the girl as well,' her mother laughed.

'Of course not. But Ted's different, Mum. You must know that.'

Fanny stared at her daughter for a long moment. 'Are you sure this isn't a case of the green-eyed monster, love?'

'Certainly not!'

'I know you'd like to be married, and now Ted's paying attention to Ada again, it's only natural if you feel envious.'

'Not in the least, I assure you, Mum. I'm only thinking of her, that's all.'

'We'll leave it at that, then, shall we? If it does work out that young Ted says anything to her about marriage, it'll be up to her to speak up. She's a grown woman, Millie; we can't interfere, not you, not me. At the end of the day it's for each of us to decide the path we'll take.'

*　★　★

After tea, when she should have been marking the older pupils' compositions, Millie set out for a walk. She needed to clear her head. Was there anything in what her mother had said, she wondered?

Having searched her conscience, she decided that she was not guilty. No, her only idea in all this was to protect her sister from making the biggest mistake of her life. The only way to deal with Ted Cooke was for Ada to meet someone new, and at least be seen to be walking out with him.

Surely there were eligible young men up at the Hall? A footman, say, or one of the outdoor servants. But if anything like that had been in the wind, they would have heard about it by now. And if Ada did have a sweetheart nearby, surely she would have run to him in her time of trouble, rather than rushing across country in the dark to reach her parents.

Her parents! Now that was an idea. In his line of work, Dad must come across plenty of young men among the estate workers. Could he be persuaded to bring one of them home for tea?

Or what about their brother, Peter? Surely he was entitled to get leave from the army, and it was many months since he'd paid them a visit. Why shouldn't he bring a comrade to Pennington Parva? She would write to him tonight, suggesting that.

But that could take months to accomplish, and in the meantime Ted was on the spot. She had to come up with something else.

Was it possible that the young doctor had fallen for Ada? Millie had heard that doctors were not allowed to have anything to do with their female patients other than the approved medical visits, but there was an answer to that. If he wished to ask Ada out, he could have simply turned her case over to Dr Atwood, and everything would be above board.

What if Ada were to marry Dr Edwin Carson? Socially, it would be a step up for the girl, and it would certainly solve all her problems.

Suddenly all the brightness had gone out of the day. It was as if a cloud had blown across the sun. Millie tried to pinpoint the source of her gloom, only to realise something which had been at the back of her mind for quite some time now.

She was falling in love with Dr Edwin Carson.

10

Abel Baker beamed at his daughter, who was sitting beside the fire, with her feet up on a stool. 'Well, well! This is a nice surprise. How are you feeling, love?'

'The doctor said she could come downstairs, just as long as she doesn't put any weight on that bad foot,' his wife told him. 'He said he won't need to be back again.'

'Thank goodness,' Ada grumbled.

'Oh, Ada. I thought you liked that young chap. He's been kind to you, and that you can't deny.'

'That's as maybe, Mum, but every time he comes it adds a few shillings to the bill. I dread to think how much that will be, when it comes.'

'It's worth it if he's managed to put you right again,' Abel said. 'When I saw the state of you when you came home that night I was afeared you'd never walk well again, if not something worse.'

'I know, Dad, and I am grateful. What worries me is how I'm going to pay. I don't have all that much saved up, and what I do have I can't get at.'

'What do you mean, love?'

'Because it's under the mattress in my old room at the Hall, that's what.'

There was silence for a while, as her parents mulled this over. 'Don't you worry, love, we'll help you,' Abel said at last, although Ada knew that he had little to spare. 'I've heard that they have doctor's clubs in some places,' he went on. 'I wish we had the like of that here.'

Fanny frowned. 'What good would that do us, then? Besides, Dr Atwood has a decent house. Why would he need a club to go to as well?'

'No, no, you don't understand. It's a scheme where folks pay in a penny a week, or some such,' Abel explained. 'Insurance, they call it. If you fall sick, it pays the doctor's bill.'

'Sounds daft to me,' Fanny said. 'You might as well keep those pennies under the mattress, the same as Ada says.'

'I don't think it works like that, love.' He tried to explain the principle behind the idea, but his wife still did not understand. He made up his mind to broach the subject with the young doctor. That still wouldn't help Ada now, but who knew what the future might hold for any of them?

That evening, when surgery hours were over, he presented himself to the doctors' house. He was rather relieved to find that Dr Atwood was out on a call. The older man was a fine doctor, but set in his ways. Abel didn't want his idea dismissed before he had even got the words out of his mouth. Fortunately Dr Carson had heard of such schemes before, and reacted to Abel's suggestion enthusiastically.

'I've had such a notion in mind for some time, Mr Baker. It's not only beneficial to the patient himself, but to us doctors as well. People tend to think that we're rolling in money, but I can't tell you how many times we don't receive anything for our trouble because the patient just cannot pay.'

Abel hadn't thought of that, but he could see how the problem worked both ways. 'So you think we should try to start up a club, then, doctor? We could call it the Jubilee medical club, in honour of the old queen's Jubilee.'

'A fine idea, and I'm sure Her Majesty would approve. Firstly, though, it's Dr Atwood we must convince. I'll have a word with him tonight and let you know later what he says about it.'

Abel walked home, feeling more cheerful than he had been since Ada's unhappy experience. On the way he met one of the farm labourers, and he couldn't resist sharing his grand idea with the fellow, but his face fell when the old man rejected it out of hand.

'I never heard such a load of tripe, Abel Baker! I don't know what you be thinking of. I've paid my way all my life, and I don't want no charity now.'

'It's not charity, Seth!' Abel countered. 'And don't tell me you wouldn't have liked to be part of a such a scheme last winter, when your Ethel came down with the cough. Dr Atwood had to see to her more than once, never mind giving her a bottle of jollop.'

'It still don't seem right to me. Say you pays in, and you never draws out. What happens to your money then, eh? Goes to line the doctor's pockets, I'll be bound. No, no, I works hard enough for my bit of money, and what I gets, I'll keep. Good day to you.'

The old man stumped off, leaving Abel feeling foolish. Still, he wouldn't give up the idea yet. Some of the younger men might be more go-ahead and the scheme might yet catch on.

He wondered if he should ask the doctors to speak to Basil Pennington. If the lord of the manor sponsored the plan, perhaps even agreeing to administer the money, people might have more faith in it.

'Don't rush your fences,' he warned

himself. In his mind, the plan ought to be voluntary, but what if Pennington decided to make obligatory payments the rule, as a condition of taking part? That could cause hardship for farm labourers with large families. Some of them had enough trouble making ends meet as it was.

He trudged on, deep in thought.

★　★　★

Meanwhile, his daughter Ada, whose difficulty had spawned his great idea, had a visitor . . .

'Who asked you to come here?' she muttered, indignation written all over her pretty face. 'You're the last person I want to see, Ted Cooke!'

'Don't be like that, Ada. Seems to me you should be thanking me for all the flowers I've brought you. And what about that bag of bullseyes; eh?'

'If I wanted bullseyes I'd buy them myself. Anyway, I prefer pear drops.'

'Pear drops, is it? Right! Then that's

what I'll bring you next time.'

'Who says there'll be a next time? P'raps I'll tell Mum not to let you in.'

'I know I made a mistake before, Ada, but I can explain,' Ted pleaded. 'Just give me a chance, won't you? We all make mistakes.'

'All right. You can have five minutes, and then go. I have to soak my foot, and if you think I'm going to let you see my ankles, you've got another think coming. Mum, could you leave us alone for a bit, please?'

Grumbling, Fanny went outside to the vegetable garden, where she filled her apron with broad beans and young carrots. She strained her ears to hear what was going on inside the kitchen, but all was quiet.

'Get on with it then!' Ada snapped, by way of encouragement.

'You know I love you . . . ' Ted began, stumbling over his words.

'You have a fine way of showing it, then! Talked about putting a ring on my finger you did, and the next thing I knew, someone came and said you'd been seen walking out with Jenny! That was a low blow, Ted Cooke, and if Jenny hadn't been sensible enough to drop you like a hot coal, who knows what might have come of it all?'

'I was fed up with never seeing you, Ada. You only had half a day off a week, and just one Sunday a month.'

'And what was I supposed to do about that? You knew I was in service when you first asked me out.'

'Ah, but you didn't give me much encouragement when I talked about us getting engaged. If you had, I'd have stayed faithful, Ada. It was only when I thought you weren't interested that I took up with Jenny.'

'And she saw right through you, so now you've come crawling back to me. Is that it, Ted?'

'Naw. I've never stopped loving you, Ada, but I thought it was no use us trying again. Then when I heard what had happened to you, I wanted to protect you. I wanted to go up to the

Hall and bash that posh chap's face.'

'But you didn't.'

'Well . . . no . . . Your Dad had already gone there and caused a stir. If I tried to put my two penn'orth in I'd never have got past the door. Honestly, though, it made me realise that I always want to protect you. I want to keep you safe for the rest of your life, Ada. Look, can't we start all over again? I promise I'll be true to you from now on.'

'I'll think about it.' Ada pouted.

'What's there to think about? Either you want me, or you don't.'

'I've said I'll think about it, and that's all you're going to get for now. Go on home with you, Ted, and don't come back until you're prepared to start again as you mean to go on.'

'But I've already said that I am.'

'Get out of here, Ted Cooke. Go!'

Bemused, he swung himself out of the door of the cottage, almost knocking Fanny over as he went.

'Well, what's got into him?' Fanny gasped, as she dropped the vegetables onto the well-scrubbed table. 'Sent him away with a flea in his ear, did you, lass?'

'Something like that, Mum.'

Fanny saw the dreamy look in Ada's eyes, and she pounced. 'Here, what's going on? You haven't taken him back, I hope!' She pursed her lips when no answer came. Surely the girl hadn't done anything so stupid?

★ ★ ★

'Not him again!' When the gate creaked Fanny peered out of the kitchen window to see Ted Cooke approaching. 'Shall I send him away?'

'It's all right, Mum. I may as well hear what he has to say.'

'Don't fall for his sweet talk, that's what I say.'

'You can play gooseberry if you like,' Ada offered. 'Then he won't say anything out of turn.'

'I'll do nothing of the sort. I've got work to be getting on with,' Fanny replied. 'Just don't do anything stupid, lass.'

'No, Mum,' Ada said, rolling her eyes impatiently.

Fanny flung the door open. 'Oh, it's you, is it? I suppose you'd better come in, then.'

'Thanks, Mrs B,' Ted answered cheerily.

'And don't call me that — it's Mrs Baker to you, my lad. And how is it you're here at this hour of the morning? Funny sort of business your dad must be running if you can go gallivanting all over the place on a weekday.'

'I'm on my way to make a delivery at Overton. Thought I'd just pop in to say hello, like.'

Fanny bustled off, leaving her daughter to deal with Ted. Ada looked at him, unsmiling. He pulled up a stool and sat down beside her.

'I was wondering if you'd like to come to the Jubilee celebrations with me. You must be getting fed up, stuck inside all day.'

'Oh, yes? And how do suggest I get there? Am I supposed to hop all the way up to Long Acre field, leaning on you, or do you mean to take me in Dad's wheelbarrow?'

He grinned. 'I would if I had to, but it won't come to that. Dad says we can have the horse and cart. What do you say to that, then?'

'What's the point? I can hardly have a go on the swing boats, can I?'

'P'raps not, but I thought you'd like to see the kiddies doing their bit, with the display they're putting on, and the races afterwards.'

'Well . . . I suppose . . . '

'And then there's a dance in the tithe barn at night. We could go to that.'

'I won't be dancing for some time to come, if ever, Ted Cooke.' Ada frowned once more. 'Or have you forgotten?'

'You could sit and watch. It would be an outing for you.'

'I've no doubt it would be. I'd see you shaking a foot with every other girl in sight, but I'd play wallflower. That's just about your style, Ted Cooke.'

'I wouldn't dance with anyone, not even the ladies' choice. I swear it, Ada. I'd sit with you and bring you lemonade. I can't say fairer than that.'

'I'll have to see.' Ada was wavering now. She would have said more but a shrill whinny came from outside, and Ted stood up.

'I'll have to go. Old Brownie's getting tired of standing. Don't forget what I said, though. You put on your best bib and tucker, and I'll come for you after dinner on Thursday.'

No sooner had the door closed behind Ted than Fanny was downstairs in a flash. 'So? What did he have to say for himself this time?'

'He wants to take me to the Jubilee celebrations, Mum. Miller Cooke is going to let us have the cart. I thought I might go . . . what do you think?'

'I don't suppose it can do any harm. An outing will do you good and the whole village will be there. It won't commit you to anything, will it?'

Ada said nothing.

'Well, will it? Answer me, Ada Baker.'

'Oh, Mum. I don't know what to do. I know I've only to say the word and we'll be back courting again, but I don't know if he's to be trusted, and that's the truth of the matter. I can do without any more heartbreak.'

'And I don't know how to advise you, love. Sometimes we just have to take a chance and see where it leads. Ted is a nice enough lad, and he's got good prospects. He'll inherit the mill in time and you'd want for nothing. I know he let you down before, and it was wrong of him to take up with that Jenny while you still had hopes of him, but we all make mistakes. I'd say he's learned his lesson now.'

'Our Millie won't like it if I let Ted back into my life. She's dead set against him, you know.'

'She's only thinking of you, love. Don't you worry about Millie. But you'd better be certain this is what you want, before you get in too deep.

Marriage is for life, and don't you forget it.'

A tear ran down Ada's cheek. 'I love him, Mum. Even after he left me for Jenny I couldn't get him out of my mind. The only reason I've been holding him at arm's length now is that I don't want to make things too easy for him, to make him earn my trust again.'

'Very right and proper, too. So you'll go with him to the celebrations?'

'Might as well.'

So when Ted stopped in on his way home some hours later, Ada was ready with her answer.

'I knew you'd say yes!' he whooped, flinging his cap in the air. 'We'll have a wonderful time, Ada, you'll see!'

'Just so you don't feel a fool, taking a cripple to the celebrations.'

'Cripple, my foot!' he shouted. 'You'll be the most beautiful girl there. All the other chaps will be jealous, that I do know. I can't wait for everyone to see us together again.'

'It's my foot, not yours,' she pointed

out with a smile, but he was so thrilled that he missed the point of her little joke completely.

* * *

Millie, meanwhile, was taking her pupils through a final rehearsal. In theory their display was simple enough that little preparation was necessary, but she had been teaching long enough to realise that they had to practise until they could perform automatically.

The younger children were to dance onto the stage — if you could call a roped-off section of grass a stage — singing the old rhyme, *Boys and girls come out to play, the moon doth shine as bright as day.* After that they were to stand in formation singing other well known nursery rhymes.

Unfortunately Miss Powell had been rather more ambitious with the older children, who were to perform madrigals.

'I wish I'd never started this,' she

sighed to Millie. 'Johnny Baxter has a voice like a fog horn and he keeps blaring out at all the wrong moments and sending the girls into fits of giggles. The problem is that I'd never hear the last of it if I kept him out of the choir. He has one of those mothers who turns up at the school in a flash if she feels her little darling is being slighted.'

'Tell him to keep quiet and just mouth the words,' Millie suggested.

'Yes, it may come to that. I'll make him stand in the back row, and hope that Nellie Baxter doesn't notice a thing.'

'If I know Mrs Baxter, she'll be too busy trying to impress all the gentry, sidling up to them in the tea tent and gushing compliments all over them.'

'That won't get her far with Lady Augusta, or Miss Julia, come to that.'

'Is Lady Augusta coming? I can't see her mixing with the peasants.'

'Oh, she's agreed to present the prizes. For the races, you know. And each child is to receive a Jubilee souvenir, something they can treasure all their lives, and show to their grandchildren in years to come. It will be many a long day before England sees another Diamond Jubilee, if ever.'

Millie thought about this. Even when she had been a pupil in this very same school, she had thought of Queen Victoria as being a very old lady, the mother of grown-up children, and a grandmother.

Their headmaster had rolled out a map of the world, taken from that very same map cupboard which had been Miss Powell's undoing, and shown them the limits of Victoria's domains. 'Just imagine, children, all the bits that are coloured in pink belong to the Empire.'

Millie had been properly impressed.

It was time now to ring the bell that would bring the children in from playtime. Would it be terrible if she gave them just one more minute? They were so fidgety as the day of celebration drew near. Surely it would do them good to run off some of their energy.

She looked forward to Thursday evening, when all the activities would be safely over, and the children handed over to their parents. Then she would be free to wander around the fairground, possibly in the company of Dr Edwin Carson. Her heart skipped a beat at the thought of it.

She imagined herself riding in a swing boat with him, clutching the velvety rope as they soared high above the crowd. Or would that be proper? What if any of the school governors saw them and thought she was making an exhibition of herself?

She wanted to ask Miss Powell what she thought, but she couldn't quite summon up the courage. Her relationship with the young doctor was too precious to discuss with anyone, although her secret would be out once they were seen together at the funfair.

'You're a fool, Millie Baker!' she muttered to herself. 'He's only asked you to go for a bit of a walk. That's hardly a commitment for life, is it?'

She had seen the admiration in his eyes, but that might be nothing more than the act of a man looking at a pretty girl and liking what he saw. She wished she could flirt as other girls did, but she didn't know how. All she could do was to be as pleasant as possible and hope against hope that it was enough. For she knew one thing for certain — she wanted to get to know Dr Edwin Carson better.

11

The great day came at last and Millie awoke early, dismayed to see a fine drizzle coming down. *Please don't let it rain all day*, she prayed, thinking of all the events that were planned and how they would be ruined if they were cursed with a steady rain. A marquee had been erected in case of wet weather, so that the children's performances could still be held, but what about the races, which the youngsters were so looking forward to? And it wouldn't be much fun wandering around the funfair in a downpour.

'Rain before seven, dry before eleven,' Fanny reminded her.

'And the sky was pink last night,' Ada put in. 'Besides, what's the point of worrying? It won't make any difference, one way or the other. Just enjoy having the morning off, for once in a while.'

'You are coming, aren't you, Mum?' Millie asked.

'Course I am, love. Wouldn't miss it for the world. I've been wanting to give my new hat an outing. The weather wouldn't dare to rain on that.'

Luckily their homespun weather predictions proved true and by the time Millie set off for school, the last drops had fallen. The whole world seemed bright and cheerful, with raindrops glistening on the leaves and all the flowers in bloom.

Women coming to cottage doors waved as she passed by, and children on their way to the school raced past her, dressed in their Sunday best.

'Stop running!' she called. 'You mustn't fall and get your clothes dirty!' But they only laughed and sped on. It was a holiday for all. Even the men were free for the afternoon — and as a special privilege, their pay would not be docked as a result.

Everyone was to share in the old queen's joy on this special day.

Most of the villagers weren't even born when she ascended the throne on the twenty-eighth of June, 1837. There were only one or two old-timers who recalled it clearly and they were in their element now, telling their tale to anyone who would listen — and a good few who tried not to!

Soon the children were assembled in a crocodile line, ready to set off for Long Acre field, where their parents and friends were already assembled.

'Take your distance, please,' Millie ordered, watching while each child placed his hands on the shoulders of the one in front. 'There is to be absolutely no pushing and shoving and make sure you keep your correct distance, so you don't tread on the heels of the person in front. And there's to be no talking, either; save your voices to sing with. Off we go, then,' she said, and the column began to move.

A dais had been set up in the field and the dignitaries were already in position. The Penningtons, of course;

Lady Augusta wearing a ghastly purple hat, trimmed with a mountain of petersham ribbon. The school governors were there in force and Millie quailed at the sight; Basil Pennington, looking stern; the vicar, of course, looking benevolent; Dr Atwood and two men whose names she did not know.

The villagers were out in force. Some had brought their kitchen chairs to sit on, while a few of the men were sitting on the grass, using neckerchiefs and pocket handkerchiefs to protect their Sunday suits from grass stains.

A flag pole had been put up and the union jack and the cross of St George fluttered gaily in the breeze. It might have been a scene from a painting, done by some famous artist, Millie thought. She suddenly felt proud to a part of it all, in this tiny corner of the old queen's empire.

All went well. The school's budget did not run to costumes for the pupils, but the girls in their white pinafores, freshly washed and starched for the occasion, made a pretty sight. Each boy had a small flag pinned to his shirt, each representing a different country in the empire. These had been painstakingly drawn and coloured in art class, which made a pleasant change from sketching sprigs of laurel or yew.

Then came the sports. Wheelbarrow races, where boys held a partner up by the ankles, while the other child did his best to move along on his hands. Three-legged races; the egg-and-spoon, which was popular with the girls; the fifty yard dash. Then, after Lady Augusta had graciously handed out small prizes to the winners, came the highlight of the event — the tug of war!

A cheer went up as Basil Pennington announced this, as, 'The governors versus the rest!' Not that the governors themselves took part, but he beckoned to a number of onlookers, who responded readily enough. James Pennington assembled an equal number of farm workers, and in this manner two teams were drawn up. After a long struggle the contest was won by 'the rest' to the accompaniment of loud cheers.

'We're off duty now, thank goodness,' Miss Powell remarked. 'The parents can look after the children now. I need a cup of tea and a long sit-down. Shall we go to the tea tent before the queue becomes too long?'

'I wonder if I may be needed to hand out the buns and lemonade for the children?' Millie wondered, but Miss Powell shook her head.

'The church ladies have it all in hand. You've done splendidly, Millie, training the children for today and coping with the whole school while I've been recovering from my accident, and I intend to tell the governors so. Now run along and enjoy yourself. I can manage without you.'

Millie's face turned pink with pleasure. Leaving Miss Powell to join a group of friends, she went in search of her mother, whom she found sitting in the shade of a tree, fanning herself. 'The children did well, dear. You've done wonders with them, I must say.'

'That's what Miss Powell said,' Millie told her mother. 'She was very complimentary about the way I've handled things.'

'And I should think so, too,' Fanny said. 'You've worked so hard these last few weeks, dear.'

'Where's Dad?' Millie asked, looking around. 'Didn't he come?'

'No. He's saving himself for the cricket match on Saturday, he said. He was afraid he'd get roped in for the tug-of-war and do himself a mischief. He's not as young as he used to be, or so he tells me.'

Millie laughed, but she sensed the fear behind her mother's words. Abel Baker's ability to work made all the difference between comfort and poverty, but his job involved tramping about the estate at all hours, in all winds and weathers. If he hurt himself and could no longer work, it would be disaster for their family. Her own meagre income could not provide for them all.

'Fetch us a cup of tea, will you?' Fanny went on. 'It's thirsty work, watching them races. And a bite of something to eat, if it's going; a nice cucumber sandwich, say, and a bit of fruit cake. That'll go down a treat.'

As Millie took her place in the queue, her eyes searched the crowd, hoping to see Dr Carson, but he was nowhere in sight. Someone tugged at her sleeve and she whirled round, hoping to see him standing there, but it was her old friend, Rose Taylor, holding little Ivy Rose by the hand.

'Well hello, Ivy Rose. Walking now, are you? No more prams for you, I see.' The child buried her face in her mother's skirts.

'I want to get her used to walking while the going's good,' Rose explained. 'I'm expecting again, so the perambulator will be needed for the next one. And what about you, Millie? I see you don't have a young man in tow yet. Not like your Ada, eh?'

'Whatever do you mean, Rose?'

'Don't play coy with me, Millie Baker! I know Ted's back with your sister, for he told me so himself.'

'First I've heard of it, then.' Millie was afraid it was true, but she was still hoping that Ada would see sense and move on.

'And there they are now!' Rose cried, waving an arm in the direction of the lane. To her dismay, Millie saw the miller's delivery cart, with Ted Cooke at the reins. Ada was seated beside him, wearing her new hat and beaming all over her face.

As Millie watched, a trio of girls ran up to greet the pair. 'Them's the maids from the Hall,' Rose said. 'Ada's work friends. Of course, she won't be having much more to do with them now, on account of she won't be going back to work up there.'

'Oh, I don't think anything's been settled yet. The doctor won't let her put too much weight on her bad foot at the moment.' Millie wasn't about to let slip that Ada was very much persona non grata with the Penningtons.

'That's not what I meant. I'm thinking our Ted wouldn't let her go back to work at all, not once they're married. It wouldn't be fitting.'

'Married?' Millie was astounded.

'Well, yes. Mind you, it's not all cut and dried, for I don't think he's summoned up the courage to actually propose yet. But his mother told my mum that he's all set to speak to Ada — and sooner rather than later.'

'I see,' Millie murmured, as the line shifted forward. 'It's been lovely seeing you, Rose, but Mum's gasping for a cup of tea and I have to go.'

'See you at the wedding, then!' Rose told her gaily.

★   ★   ★

The school governors retired to the rectory for their meeting. Since they had all been present to watch the children's activities, it seemed sensible to hold their regular meeting afterwards, rather than

145

returning another day. They were all busy men and, as one of them often said, time was money.

Because this was a Church of England school, the vicar acted as chairman. Each item on the agenda was quickly dispensed with, but when he asked the ritual question, 'Any other business?' he was surprised when Dr Atwood spoke up.

'Yes, Mr Chairman. I wish to discuss the proposed health club.'

'Oh, not now,' Basil Pennington groaned. 'Surely that can wait? I really must get back to pick up my wife. She doesn't like to be kept waiting.'

'That is unfortunate, but the sooner we begin on this, the sooner we'll be finished. Surely Lady Augusta won't mind waiting for a few minutes if what we decide will benefit the whole community? I'm sure she has the good of the people at heart.'

'Oh, very well — get on with it, man.'

'For the benefit of those who have yet to hear of the scheme — Mr Francis and Mr Boddy — it has been proposed that we instigate a club which will help people meet their doctor's-bills in time of need.'

'Ah, so this is for your benefit, Atwood.'

'Of course it means that we should receive our just dues, Mr Boddy, but that isn't the point. Look at it this way . . . someone with an ailing child, for example, or a wife with a lengthy illness, possibly leading to death, can be left with debts he cannot possibly pay, which can lead to real hardship. These medical clubs have been tried in other places with some success. Families pay in a small sum on a regular basis, and in time of need their medical bill is covered.'

'You mean even when the total sum is greater than they've paid in?'

'That's the idea.'

'It'll never work, man!' Mr Boddy argued. 'Say the others in the club pay in, week after week, but they all keep good health and never need to draw out any money. Think of the resentment it will cause when they see some other chap reaping the benefit. No, no. Let each man provide for his own, I say. Let him salt away a few pennies here and there, and all will be well.'

'Until the rents go up, or there's a poor harvest,' Dr Atwood countered. 'And it's goodbye to their savings — but this way their money will be safe. What I'm proposing is a sort of insurance policy, you see. The plan will be strictly voluntary, so those who prefer to keep their cash in their pockets are free to go their own way.'

Basil Pennington frowned. 'It seems to me there's a flaw in all this. Say those men pay in for a few weeks and then a diphtheria epidemic comes along. There won't be enough in the kitty to cover expenses if they all want to draw out at once.'

'A good point, Pennington, and that's where we come in,' Dr Atwood replied instantly. 'I propose that each of the school governors should donate a lump sum to get the scheme off to a good start.'

'Steady on, old chap!' Silas Boddy objected. 'What sort of lump sum are we talking about, exactly?'

'Anything you care to give, Boddy. As for myself, I have already pledged a portion of my stipend. Surely we can all do the same? What about you, Pennington?' Dr Atwood turned his gaze on Basil Pennington.

'I think I've already done quite enough in the way of charity. My cook has just managed to scald herself quite badly, which is most inconvenient. We had to call the doctor to her. Then a guest in our home — a college friend of my son — had an accident and I felt honour bound to stump up, since he wasn't able to pay. You know what students are like.'

'And, no doubt,' Dr Atwood raised one eyebrow, 'you'll be underwriting Miss Baker's bill, as well.'

'What? What about Miss Baker?'

'I understand from my junior partner

that she was employed in your house when she was attacked by that same college friend of young James. In running to the safety of her own home she incurred injuries which might preclude her ever going into service again. I'm sure you agree that such a decent young woman also deserves to be helped.'

This was news to Boddy and Francis, who leaned forward, looking avidly at Basil Pennington, who blustered, 'Of course, I shall bear it in mind.' No doubt the story would be all round the county by morning; he knew the pair had never liked him. He must stop the rot before it was too late.

'I shall give one hundred pounds to start things rolling,' Pennington announced, 'in honour of the Queen's Jubilee — on condition that the scheme be known as the Lady Augusta Pennington Medical Club. My wife has the welfare of our tenants very much at heart and would appreciate the little honour.'

'That is most generous of you,' the

vicar gushed, looking around at his fellow governors, several of whom nodded vigorously.

Mr Boddy sniffed. 'Should the thing not be called the Jubilee fund, then? Or even the Diamond? After all, this is the Queen's Diamond Jubilee year.'

'Certainly, Boddy, if we are all going to contribute. Can we expect you to match my donation, then?'

The men all looked at each other in consternation. One hundred pounds was a great deal of money — several years' wages for a working man. While they were all well-to-do, they had not reached their current standard of living by throwing good money about. In the case of the vicar, he had nothing but his stipend and his living was in the hands of Basil Pennington, whose right it was to appoint the vicars in this parish and, presumably, to complain about them to the bishop if they did not give satisfaction.

He hastened to the rescue. 'We live here in Pennington Parva. Surely it is right that the organization should reflect the Pennington name? And if it pays tribute to Lady Augusta, all the better. I believe that our gracious Queen would approve.'

Basil inclined his head with a smile. 'We shall, of course, need a reliable person to administer the thing. You will be too busy, vicar, with your parish duties, and as for you, Atwood, it would be best if you were seen to operate at arm's length, since you will be the ultimate recipient of any revenues. I nominate Silas Boddy to take charge of this.'

'I accept.' Boddy stood up and bowed. Pennington was the only man present who knew he harboured secret yearnings to stand for Parliament some day, and being associated with such a public charity would do him no harm at all. 'No time like the present. If we are all in agreement I shall make an announcement at the dance tonight, since most of the villagers will be there, I expect.'

'If I may make a suggestion?' the

vicar murmured. 'Make the announcement by all means, but do not attempt to explain how it will all work. Say that a meeting will be held at a later date for that purpose. Tonight's dance is a happy occasion, to round off the celebrations and people will be in no mood to listen to this sort of thing — no matter how beneficial the club may be to them in the long run.'

★ ★ ★

When Basil Pennington returned to his wife's side, he could see that she was very annoyed indeed. Besieged on all sides by eager women who wanted to be able to say that they had actually met the lady of the manor on social terms, she was using her fan in an agitated manner.

'Where have you been, Basil? I've been ready to leave this past half hour. I would have gone away and left you to walk home, except that Snead is nowhere to be found. I've a good mind to give him his marching orders.'

'I told Snead he could go and have a look around until I sent for him, dear. I imagine he's in the tea tent or having a chat with his cronies.'

'Then for goodness' sake, Basil, send for him now. I'm quite worn out with talking to all these boring people for the entire afternoon,' she sighed.

Her husband snapped his fingers at a passing boy, who jumped to attention at once, hoping no doubt, to earn a farthing for running an errand.

'Do you know my coachman, Thomas Snead, boy?'

'Oh, yes, sir! He's my mother's uncle, or summink of that sort.'

'I don't need the man's life history, boy! Run along and find him. Tell him his master wants him. Be quick about it.'

'Yes, sir. Right away, sir.' The child sped off.

'And now I suppose we stand here for another half hour, while Snead is run to ground!' Augusta grumbled. 'I don't know why I ever agreed to attend these rural high jinks. What a waste of a fine afternoon.'

'Never mind that. Just wait until I tell you what's about to happen. You're being given a singular honour, my dear. A charitable fund is being set up to aid the sick of the parish, and it will bear your name. Now then, what do you think about that?' he asked, pleased with himself.

'And how much did that cost you, Basil?' she sniffed in reply.

12

Millie was in seventh heaven. She was strolling through the fairground, accompanied by Dr Edwin Carson. He had suddenly appeared at her side, smiling, and asking if he might join her, and she had been delighted to agree. Now the garish delights of the rides and the sideshows seemed tinged with magic, and the music of the roundabouts and the shrieks of happy children all added to the excitement of the evening.

'I think I'll try the hoopla,' she murmured. 'It looks easy. All you have to do is throw a hoop over one of those prizes, and it's yours.'

'Ah, but do you see those blocks the prizes are standing on? The hoop has to go over those as well, and settle down flat on the stall. It's hard to do. I'd save your money, if I were you.'

'Then I'll have a go at the coconut

shy instead. I've never tasted coconut.' But after hurling the three balls at the giant nuts, perched on poles, she had failed to win one. Frustrated, she paid for three more balls, with the same result.

'Oh, bother!' she cried, laughing. 'You have a go, Doctor.'

'Please call me Edwin,' he told her. We're walking out now, Millie — no need to be so formal.'

Suddenly overcome with joy, Millie smiled up at him tenderly. He had said it! They were 'walking out'. This put their relationship on an official footing. Her whole being flooded with happiness.

Edwin returned her smile warmly. 'I'd rather try my luck at the shooting range. I'm used to grouse shooting, so downing a few clay pigeons should pose no problem.'

The stall holder regarded the doctor glumly. Still, if this chap won a prize it would encourage the others. The evidence of their own eyes was worth all his patter. 'Roll up, roll up!' he shouted. 'Win a prize for the lady, mister!'

True to his word, Edwin won a prize, a celluloid doll which he promptly presented to Millie. 'Here's a souvenir for you, Millie. It's come a few years too late for you to play with, but you can always put it by for your children.'

'Oh, Mith! What a beautiful dolly!'

Millie looked down to see one of her smallest pupils gazing at the cheap toy, her little hands clasped in ecstasy.

'Hello, Sally. Enjoying yourself, are you?'

'Yeth, Mith.' The child's tongue protruded through the gap in her teeth.

'Have you been on the carousel? I fancy a ride on a black horse, myself.'

'No, Mith. I ain't got no money.'

'You haven't any money,' Millie said, instinctively correcting her.

'Thath what I said, Mith.'

Millie sighed. 'Then I suppose you'd better have this dolly to play with instead. Look after her well, now and don't let your big brother anywhere near her. If I know Freddy Styles he'll have her head off in no time.'

'Oh, thanks you, Mith!' The look in the child's eyes as she accepted the doll meant the world to Millie.

Edwin pulled his hand out of his pocket as the child ran off and asked Millie, 'Why did you shake your head just now? I was about to give the girl a penny or two so she'd have something to spend.'

'It wouldn't have been fair,' she explained. 'Word would have flown round and the other children would have wanted to know why young Sally was favoured over them. It might even have led to resentment among the parents. Giving her the doll was all right, you see, because she's a child, and dolls are made for little girls.'

'Honestly, Millie! All this fuss over tuppence.'

She shook her head. 'Easy to tell you're not used to life in the country, Edwin. They're proud people here and you have to treat them all alike, or not at all. If you mean to stay here in Pennington Parva you need to take note of people's sensibilities, don't you see?'

She stopped suddenly, wondering if she'd spoken out of turn. Men didn't like women who set themselves up to know best — or so Fanny had always told her. They wanted wives who would defer to them. But it seemed that Edwin had taken her words to heart, for he nodded gravely.

'And would you like me to stay in Pennington Parva, Millie Baker?' he enquired. Millie blushed, but said nothing. 'Come on, then, let's go and have a look at the swing boats,' he said, taking her by the hand.

★   ★   ★

Standing in the shadows beside the hot chestnut stall, Julia Pennington scowled. Who did that little school mistress think she was, making an exhibition of herself like that, going hand-in-hand with the doctor in a public place? If they actually went on the swing boats, it would provide her with some ammunition to go to Papa. She could get the silly chit dismissed, and serve her right, too. Why on earth Edwin Carson should be interested in the gamekeeper's daughter when he could be squiring the beautiful Miss Pennington around was beyond understanding.

Julia wondered how she could turn the situation to her advantage. She could hardly walk up to the man and tell him to get rid of the girl and pay attention to her instead! An idea came to her then, and she laughed softly. All was not lost . . .

★　★　★

Midsummer Day was only just past, and it would be ten o'clock or later before darkness fell. However, it was already dark in the windowless tithe barn when Edwin and Millie followed the crowd there. The dance was supposed to begin at eight o'clock and

161

the building was fast filling up. Lanterns had been lit, giving the place a romantic glow, and musicians were already tuning up, ready to accompany the dancing. There were fiddles and flutes, as well as a big bass drum.

'What's that for?' Millie wondering, turning to Edwin. 'If they bang on that it will drown out all the rest.'

'I expect it's to get attention when the master of ceremonies wants to make an announcement,' he explained. Sure enough, a volley of sound drew their attention to Silas Boddy, who was one of the school governors, as Millie knew. She hoped he wasn't going to ruin things with some long, dreary speech. Basil Pennington had already praised the childrens' performance earlier in the day, so it could not be that.

'It is my privilege to announce the inauguration of a medical club for the benefit of you all,' Boddy declared. 'Some of you know from experience how hard it is to find the money to pay your doctors' bills. Those days are gone forever, with the help of Mr Basil Pennington, who has kindly established a fund for the purpose, in honour of the Diamond Jubilee, to be known as the Lady Augusta Pennington Medical Club. A meeting will be held at a later date to explain this further.'

Uncertain of what this was all about, but recognising that some response was required, people began to clap. Millie turned to Edwin in great indignation. 'That was your idea, Edwin. Why should the Penningtons get all the glory?'

'I don't think it matters whose idea it was, so long as people get the help they need. Besides, we don't know any of the details yet. Let's wait until the meeting before we jump to conclusions. If people don't agree with what's proposed, I shan't mind if the idea can't be traced back to me.'

'Dr Carson! Fancy finding you here. Do you mean to dance?'

Edwin swung around to see Julia Pennington, dressed in a royal blue gown, created in the latest fashion and much too ornate for a country hop. She looked through Millie as if she wasn't there.

'Miss Julia, good evening. Have you been enjoying the fun of the fair?'

Julia curled her lip. 'Hardly. Can you see me riding a wooden horse on a roundabout, when I've the real thing in our stables?'

'No, I suppose not, but no doubt you'll enjoy the dancing.'

'Don't be foolish, Dr Carson. I've no wish to have this gown pawed over by village men with grubby hands. No, I've been looking for you to pass on a message. A boy came with the request that you attend upon old Mrs Cole. She is on her deathbed, apparently.'

'I'm off duty tonight and Dr Atwood is on call. I'll pass the message on to him immediately,' Edwin replied politely.

'The boy was insistent that the woman wanted you.'

'Very well,' Edwin sighed and turned to Millie. 'I'm so sorry, Millie . . . '

'Of course, Edwin, I understand.'

'Did the boy say if the vicar has been summoned? He'll have to be there.'

Julia shrugged. 'I'd go to the rectory if I were you. If the vicar hasn't left, you can go in the pony cart with him. The Coles' smallholding is miles away. It would be a long ride on a bicycle.'

Regretfully, Millie watched as Edwin dashed down the lane towards the rectory. Why, oh why, did the poor old soul have to pick tonight of all nights to pass away?

★   ★   ★

All eyes were on Ada as she hobbled into the barn, with her right arm around Ted's neck for support. As he settled her on a bench where she could sit and see everything that was going on, she was immediately surrounded by a group of young women. Some were girls she'd gone to school with, who knew the story of her on-off-on-again relationship with Ted Cooke, others were fellow maids from the Hall, who had been given the evening off in honour of the Jubilee celebrations.

'Is this your young man, then?' Susan asked eagerly.

Ada smiled, but did not reply.

Ted turned to join his friends. 'I'll be back when I can get a look-in,' he told Ada in amusement.

'Have you heard about Mrs Beasley?' Susan asked, going on to tell the story of how the cook had upset a pan of boiling water all over her legs. Screamed summink awful, her did. Just about brought the house down.'

'When are you coming back, then?' Annie wanted to know.

'Don't know as I am. It all depends,' Ada replied cryptically.

'Depends on what?'

Once more Ada gave no satisfaction, but the omission wasn't noted because the other girl gave a shriek, hastily suppressed. 'Isn't that Miss Julia over there in the doorway? What's she doing here?'

'The Penningtons have been here most of the day,' Ada said. 'Making speeches and giving out prizes. I thought they'd all gone home by now.'

'And so they should. It's bad enough having to work in their house without them watching us when we're off duty. Just look at Miss Julia in that gown. The cost of that would keep a poor family for a year.'

As they watched, James Pennington took his sister by the arm and drew her outside. 'The pony trap is waiting, if you want to go home,' he informed her. 'Should I ask Snead to wait, or tell him to go back?'

'I might as well go home. There's nothing to keep me here. I'm surprised to see you still here, though.'

'Oh, the pater told me to come. He thinks it would be a good idea for me to trip the light fantastic with the village maidens. Something to remember in their old age, or nonsense like that. Telling their grandchildren how they danced with the young master at Queen

Victoria's Diamond Jubilee.'

'Then just be careful you don't follow Eustace Savage-Rowe's example. That really would put the cat among the pigeons.'

'As if I would! A chaste kiss in the moonlight is about my limit. Unlike old Eustace, I have to live here, at least for part of the year,' James replied.

'Then I advise you to stay away from Baker. She's sitting over there, wearing a face that would stop a clock.'

'Baker?' He looked confused.

'You know very well who I mean. She's the maid who caused all the trouble with Eustace.'

'Right-ho! I'll steer well clear. So, are you going, or not? I take it there's nobody here who's taken your fancy.' James laughed good-naturedly.

'Mind your own business!' Julia snapped, flouncing away.

Millie watched her go. She hadn't liked the sly smile she had noticed on Miss Julia's face when Edwin had left to attend his patient. No doubt she was delighted that Millie's evening had been ruined, but could there have been more to it? It had appeared at first that the girl intended to stay around, ready to greet Edwin on his return, but now she seemed to be leaving, and that was all to the good.

Ada was still surrounded by well-wishers, and gossip-mongers, eager to learn about the goings on at the Hall. More than one young man asked Millie to dance, but she refused kindly, saying she was tired out after the day's activities and wished to go home and rest. Having said that, she would have to leave soon, or risk getting a reputation for being uppity.

Sadly she strolled home through the gathering gloom. The lights were on in the cottage when she arrived home and she found her mother in the kitchen, stitching away at some garment-in-progress.

'Hello, love. Have a good time, did you?'

'Yes, thank you.'

'You don't look as if you did! Nobody asked you to dance, then?'

'Oh, one or two. I was too tired though, so I've come home to go to bed.'

'Worn out with coaching the kiddies for the displays, I suppose. I thought it all went very well. I stayed for a bit, but then I had to come back to get your dad's tea. I wish I could have brought him some of those cakes, but I didn't like to ask. I've never seen such an assortment all in one place.'

Millie sat down suddenly and sighed unhappily. 'Oh, Mum, why do some people have to be so horrible?'

'Has somebody said something to upset you, love?'

'Not exactly. It's Miss Julia . . . '

'Oh, yes? What's she done now?'

'It's just that Dr Carson — Edwin — well, he seems to like me, Mum.'

'And you like him?'

Tears came in to Millie's eyes. 'Yes, I really do.'

'And that Julia's got her eye on him,

has she? Well, all's fair in love and war, isn't that what they say? You must stand up to her and if you and the young doctor are meant to be together, that's the way it will be.'

'But she's got everything, Mum. Beauty, money, lovely clothes. I can't possibly compete with all that.'

'Handsome is as handsome does,' Fanny quoted unhelpfully.

'I'm off to bed, Mum. Goodnight.'

'Goodnight, God bless, see you in the morning,' Fanny murmured, as she had done every night since her children were born.

* * *

Meanwhile, back at the dance, Ada was tiring too. 'I'm getting weary, Ted. Would you mind taking me home?'

'I will if you like, but aren't you enjoying yourself?'

'It's been lovely, but it's not much fun sitting here watching everyone else dance. I've chatted to everyone now, and there's nothing left to say.'

'Right-ho. I'll just say good night to the chaps, and then I'll go and hitch up the horse. I'll come back when it's ready, all right?'

It was delightful sitting in the cart while the horse picked its way down the rutted lane. The scent of cottage flowers drifted on the air, and a bright moon shone down on the travellers. Leaning against some grain sacks, Ada was almost lulled to sleep, but she sat up suddenly when they turned in at a farm lane, and drew to a halt.

'What are we stopping here for?'

'I thought the horse could do with a rest.'

'We've only come a mile, Ted Cooke. What are you up to?'

'I've been thinking about this all evening, Ada. You know I love you, sweetheart. Will you marry me?'

Ada hesitated. She had rehearsed this scene in her mind, over and over again. She intended to say no at first, to make him pay for his cavalier treatment of her the year before, but she had loved him since she was a schoolgirl. Some people might say she was choosing to wed him to avoid going back into service — but she didn't care. Let them say what they liked!

'Of course I'll marry you, Ted!'

Ted gasped with relief. 'I was hoping you'd say that!'

The moon shone down on the two lovers kissing and it was only when the horse moved restlessly that they drew apart and set off for the rest of the way to the gamekeeper's cottage.

'Shall I come in and speak to your Dad?' Ted asked.

'You might as well. I'll need help getting into the house.'

There were other things to say. Ted's mother, apprised of her son's plan to propose after the dance, wanted him to bring Ada to the house for Sunday tea. In the near future, of course, Fanny and Abel would have to play host to the Cookes, as the miller's future in-laws. Then the women would come into their own, as there would be talk of a date for the wedding, the making of a guest list, and what each of them would wear.

As Ada had hoped, her parents were delighted with the news, and Fanny went to break open a bottle of her best parsnip wine.

'Is Millie home?' Abel wanted to know. 'We'd better have her down to toast the bride and groom. This is a happy night indeed. Think of it, Fanny. Our first child, all set to get wed! We'll have to let the lads know at once, so they can plan to be here.'

'Better not, love. Oh, write to the boys, by all means, but let our Millie sleep. She came home that white and tired as you wouldn't believe.'

Fanny didn't know how Millie was going to take this news. She wished fervently that her younger daughter could find a man of her own, but that wouldn't be easy when Millie was such an independent spirit.

13

Red-faced, John Edmonds, vicar of St Martin's, Pennington Parva, glared at Basil Pennington. 'I really must protest!' he cried. He usually made every attempt to control his temper, as befitted a priest of the Church, but on this occasion he had been pushed too far. Nor did it concern him at this moment that his living was in the gift of the man he was confronting. 'Your daughter's action is quite reprehensible. I ask that you speak to her in the strongest possible terms, or I shall have to do it for you!' He took a step backwards, knowing he had said too much, and waited for the axe to fall.

Surprisingly, Basil Pennington only looked bewildered. 'I'm not quite sure that I understand. What exactly has the child done?'

'She sent me on a wild goose chase

out to Benjamin Cole's smallholding, and Dr Carson with me. Right out to the furthest bounds of the parish, as you must know, and all on a pretext that his old mother was about to die.'

'Are you sure, Vicar? I can hardly believe that my daughter would play such a prank! What would be her motive? Please be careful what you say.'

The clergyman cast his mind back to what had taken place. The two men had rushed out to the Cole home, forcing the vicar's poor horse to gallop all the way, and when they had entered the house it was to find old Mrs Cole sitting in a rocking chair, smoking a pipe.

'Why, it's you, Vicar,' Ben Cole had cried, 'and the young doctor! Look, Mother, it's visitors! Why are you here, gentlemen? Has there been some kind of accident?'

'We were informed that Mrs Cole was on her deathbed,' Edwin had told him. 'Naturally we came with all speed.'

The old lady cackled and puffed on her pipe. 'Me, I plan to live to be a hundred. I doubt if you'll be able to say the same. You look like you're about to have an apoplexy, Vicar, all red and gasping!'

The farmer had scratched his head, perplexed. 'I didn't send for you, gentlemen, so who did?'

'You didn't send a boy?'

'What boy? There's no boy here. All I have is a bevy of daughters, and they're more trouble than they're worth. Now, would you join me in a pint of ale, just to show there's no hard feelings?'

On the way back to the village, the vicar had questioned Edwin as to who the boy might have been.

'I have no idea for I never saw the child. It was Miss Julia who passed the message on, and naturally I believed her completely.'

'I've known that girl since the day she was born,' the vicar had said, his expression grim. 'And she'll say whatever it suits her if it means she can get her own way. Tell me this, what were you doing when she told this tale?'

'Just standing there in the doorway of the tithe barn, taking in the scene.'

'All alone, were you?' the vicar had asked.

'No, actually, I was with Miss Baker . . . Millie, that is. I've become quite fond of her, and we'd spent a happy afternoon at the celebrations.'

'Ah, that's it then!'

'What ever do you mean?'

'Julia Pennington wants you for herself, my boy. I've seen her sidling up to you after Matins, smirking all over her pretty face. It's my belief she saw you with young Millie and decided to come between you, and what a better way to do it than to say you were urgently needed by poor Mrs Cole!'

'Surely not. She'd know we'd find out we'd been made fools of.'

'Ah, but remember the mythical boy — the naughty little prankster!'

'But she heard me say I was going to fetch you, and she didn't try to stop me then. She's not in love with you as well, is she?'

The vicar had given a hollow laugh. 'That girl has disliked me ever since I complained about her galloping her horse around the graveyard, jumping him over tombstones, if you please! No, there's no love lost between me and Miss Julia Pennington, and I shall make sure her parents know what she's been up to this time.'

Now, facing Basil Pennington, John Edmonds repeated what had been said in this conversation. 'The girl must realise what could have happened in different circumstances,' he went on. 'Let us suppose that a doctor really was urgently needed, but could not be found because Dr Carson had been sent so far away. Or perhaps I was needed at a genuine deathbed, and that person had died without the comfort of his religion. Miss Julia should set an example to those less fortunate in the parish than herself, but I'm sorry to say that she shows no signs of doing that.'

'I apologise on her behalf,' Basil Pennington said, 'and you can leave it to me. I shall deal with my daughter without delay. Her mother and I have been concerned about her behaviour for some time, and we have decided to pack her off to a finishing school in Switzerland. The arrangements have already been made. There will be no more trouble, I can assure you.'

★ ★ ★

Two days later Millie was delighted to open the door to Edwin, who presented her with a large bouquet of flowers.

'I went to the school, but there was nobody there,' he announced.

'School's over until September, thank goodness. Will you come in?'

'Actually I came to invite you out to tea on Sunday, but I suppose I can step in for a moment or two.'

'Tea? You mean, for a picnic?'

'No, no. I want you to come to the doctor's house. The housekeeper has promised to bake a jam sponge, especially for the occasion.'

'How lovely! Come on, then, and say hello to Mum.'

Fanny smiled when she saw them together. 'I heard you were called out to old Mrs Cole the other night. Was she taken bad?'

'Mum, you're not supposed to ask that. Doctors can't talk about their patients.' Millie shook a finger at her mother light-heartedly.

'Easy to see you're a school mistress,' Fanny retorted spiritedly. 'You take that finger back before I bite it off!'

'There is nothing wrong with Mrs Cole,' Edwin said, trying not to laugh at their antics. 'We were sent out there on a wild goose chase, and the vicar is hopping mad about it.'

'Never! Some naughty child, I suppose,' Fanny observed.

'Actually it was Miss Julia Pennington.'

'Never!'

'And you may as well know the rest, for it's all round the village by now. She's been shipped off to a finishing school in Switzerland, so that will stop her capers,' Edwin told them.

'Seems there's one rule for the Penningtons and another for the rest of us,' Millie grumbled. 'Do things the rest of us would be punished for, and she gets sent to Switzerland! There's no justice in this world.'

'What are you talking about?' Fanny asked.

Edwin grinned at her. 'Millie will tell you all about it some time, and meanwhile I must be on my way. I'll see you on Sunday, then?'

Millie saw him to the door, and suddenly she felt as blithe as a bird that sings in the meadow from dawn until dusk. Miss Julia had been prevented from doing further harm, and all was right with the world.

*   *   *

Ada and Ted were married in the spring of 1898. Her brother, Peter, was able to get leave from the army, which made Ada very happy. Their other brother,

Jack, could not attend, for Canada was too far away and the fare to Britain too costly. However, he did send a generous gift of money, telling Ada to buy something with it for her new home.

Millie was a bridesmaid, in a pretty blue dress which could be worn again and again. Only the gentry could afford special bridal attire, to be worn only once and then discarded.

'You'll be next,' Fanny told her, beaming. 'I'll be happy for you, of course, but sad, too, to see my last babe leaving home.'

For Edwin had proposed to Millie at Christmas, saying that he wanted to become established in his profession before taking on the responsibilities of matrimony. Millie had agreed willingly. One more year of teaching would help to build their little nest egg, and she was already embroidering pillowcases and antimacassars for her bottom drawer.

'Fancy me being a doctor's wife,' she said to her mother happily.

'It won't be easy, love,' Fanny replied. 'You'll have to get used to having a husband who's likely to be called out at any hour of the day or night, and I expect that some people will come to you for advice — women who don't want to confide in a man, that is.'

'I love Edwin,' Millie said, 'and I can tackle whatever comes, as long as we're together. Just like you and Dad have done, all these years.'

Fanny smiled then with a contented heart, for it had been her experience that love conquered all.

THE END

We do hope that you have enjoyed reading this large print book.

Did you know that all of our titles are available for purchase?

We publish a wide range of high quality large print books including:
Romances, Mysteries, Classics
General Fiction
Non Fiction and Westerns

Special interest titles available in large print are:
The Little Oxford Dictionary
Music Book, Song Book
Hymn Book, Service Book

Also available from us courtesy of Oxford University Press:
Young Readers' Dictionary
(large print edition)
Young Readers' Thesaurus
(large print edition)

For further information or a free brochure, please contact us at:
Ulverscroft Large Print Books Ltd.,
The Green, Bradgate Road, Anstey,
Leicester, LE7 7FU, England.
Tel: (00 44) **0116 236 4325**
Fax: (00 44) **0116 234 0205**

JUST A MEMORY AWAY

Moyra Tarling

In hospital, Alison Montgomery cannot remember her own name. She hears the doctors' hushed whispers — sees their worried glances, which speak of the dark secrets lying just beyond the locked shutters of her memory. Then they bring her the stranger who says he's her husband. But why can't she remember loving a man as compelling as Nicholas Montgomery? And yet the shadows in his eyes clearly reveal that there's something in their past better left forgotten . . .